A WOMAN IN HIDING

A WOMAN IN HIDING

T.B. MARKINSON

Published by T. B. Markinson
Visit T. B. Markinson's official website at lesbianromancesbytbm.com for the latest news, book details, and other information.
Copyright © T. B. Markinson, 2023
Cover Design by: Erin Dameron-Hill
Edited by Kelly Hashway

This book is copyrighted and licensed for your personal enjoyment only. All rights reserved. No part of this publication may be reproduced, stored in a retrieval system, or transmitted in any forms or by any means without the prior permission of the copyright owner. The moral rights of the author have been asserted.

This book is a work of fiction. Names, characters, businesses, places, events, and incidents are the product of the author's imagination or are used fictitiously. Any resemblance to actual persons, living or dead, events, or locales is entirely coincidental.

CHAPTER ONE

"Do you know what my problem is?" I wheeled about, my flip-flops sliding on the perfectly manicured grass of our host's backyard. With only minimal arm flailing, I managed to correct course right before crashing onto my buttocks in front of the assembled crowd of children and parents who had gathered for today's birthday celebration.

"Balance? Coordination?" Sarah, my wife, counted out a list of prime suspects on her fingers. "Oh, I know. Inappropriate footwear?"

"There is nothing wrong with my footwear. Or my balance." I lifted one foot to demonstrate my balancing prowess. Almost instantly, the flip-flop slid from my foot, dropping upside down onto the slightly damp ground. I stared in dismay at the flecks of mud dotting the sole. "Can you turn it right side up for me? My fingers are going to get dirty."

Stooping to comply with my request, Sarah let out an anguished sigh that spoke volumes. It was a sound I'd heard on a regular basis over our many years together. "We're at a birthday party for a sweet six-year-old girl. Why do you look like you want to murder someone?"

"Why are you acting like I'm the issue? I'm not the problem." I placed a hand over my chest as I wriggled my toes so that the leather strap could slide into place between them. "And, you didn't answer my question."

"Trust me, Lizzie. You don't want me to start listing all your potential problems. We'll be here until next week, and while the temperatures are great today, we're expecting rain tomorrow."

"Hardy har har." I stuck out my tongue. "The answer to my very important question is I'm not mean enough."

"You think you're not—" Sarah choked on her words, her eyes bugging out of her head.

I held up a hand. "You had your chance to weigh in before. I'm telling you I'm not mean enough. That's the only correct response."

Sarah blinked rapidly as if she'd stepped out into the sun after living in a dark cave for the past two years, which given the recent COVID experience, wasn't all that far-fetched. "I don't understand what happened. I left you alone for three minutes, tops, to say hello to Sally. In that amount of time, your mood has entirely shifted, and now you think your sole problem in life is you're not mean enough? What the fu—" she corrected to "fudge happened in those three minutes?"

"I had a revelation."

Sarah acted out wanting to strangle me and then immediately checked her Fitbit. "I got three extra steps doing that. Keep it up, and I'll meet my daily goal soon."

"What's the goal, to get ten-thousand steps or actually murder me? Or, I wonder, would murdering me get you that many points?" My mind whizzed from one topic to the next, leaving me dazed, all the while questioning why I had planted those deadly thoughts in Sarah's head. Now she was staring at me like she was game to find out exactly how many calories could be burned by grasping my throat and not letting go.

"I haven't decided yet. Time will tell." While her smile was saucy, I didn't know how to interpret the shift of emotions in her dark eyes.

So I opted to do what I generally did when in doubt and ignored the murder plot thread. No sense delving too deeply. For me, the phrase *ignorance is bliss* wasn't just something to slap on the side of a coffee mug. It was my life motto. Otherwise, I was pretty sure I wouldn't make it to my fortieth birthday, which was coming up. I couldn't remember exactly when, since numbers weren't my thing, and as a historian, future dates always did my head in. Surely, Sarah would know. I could ask her, but that'd get me off track again.

What had I been trying to say?

Oh, right! We'd been talking about the source of my irritation. "I got an email from the admin in the history department asking me to fill in for another professor whose brother died."

"How sad."

"Yeah, I guess." I frowned at Sarah's apparent sincerity, fearing we were threatening to veer off topic again. "But the way the admin phrased the email, I can't say no without looking like an asshole, so I simply wrote back, *sure*."

"What else would you have said?"

The look Sarah was giving me suggested there was something going on that I was missing. I didn't like it, and my eyes quickly fell to the ground. I shifted on my feet, feeling lost. It was not an unfamiliar feeling. Minutes earlier, I really thought I'd put my finger on the single most important issue, one that had been causing me nothing but anguish for the entirety of my life. But hearing it all out loud, coupled with the expression on my wife's face, I began to fear I may have been the asshole in this situation.

"I have a more important question." A hint of softness had returned to my wife's voice, tempting me to dare looking up from the ground. "Why are you reading emails on a beautiful Saturday morning in May?"

"Because my phone dinged." I appreciated that

she'd asked an easy question, one I had a ready answer to.

"Lizzie, we're at a party. On a weekend. I feel like you're missing what's going on around you." Sarah made a gesture like a game show host with her arms, encompassing the backyard with its balloons and streamers like it was some sort of grand prize. Granted, it was a nice backyard, complete with a spacious deck and sculptures, but it was no new car.

"It's a party for Fred and Ollie's little school friend. I'm not partaking in the festivities." I waved a hand up and down in the air, calling attention to my full-grown form. "Adult."

Sarah cocked a brow. "Numerically speaking, you may qualify. Emotionally? Not even close."

Before I could deliver a fitting comeback, Sarah waved at one of the moms across the playground, flashing a *nice to see you* smile, but I wasn't fooled. She was probably imagining killing me and stuffing me into a piece of luggage to dispose of my body. I'd spent many hours during lockdown trying to figure out how to dispose of a body. No one in particular. I just found the mental exercise relaxing.

There was one problem. I never could get past how to fit a body into a piece of luggage without a bone saw. Not only didn't I own one, I feared checking them out online would get me onto at least one watch list. Another issue was I couldn't handle blood, bones, or guts.

A mental image of all three induced a full-body shiver that was completely at odds with the warm weather and probably with whatever it was we'd been talking about—not that I could recall what that was.

Sarah's watchful eyes darted to me like a homing device, and I knew I needed to think fast. Any second now, I would be spilling every single inappropriate, serial killer thought that had ever run through my mind during what I referred to as my dark moments.

"Have you noticed the rocks these people are wearing?" I asked by way of diversion. "That woman's diamond is the size of a goose egg. It could be the crown jewel of a small country. Why are we encouraging our children to play with their kids?"

I wasn't necessarily good at diversions.

"I keep telling you the kids need friends outside of the Petrie household. Moreover, I also need friends. And so do you."

Uh-oh. I'd gotten moreovered. Whenever Sarah started sounding like an English teacher, it was a bad sign for me.

That didn't stop me from saying, "I keep telling you I didn't have friends growing up, and I turned out fine." *Whatever you do, Lizzie, do not blab about the bone saw right now.*

"Says the compassionate adult who's been whining that she has to babysit a class because her colleague's brother died."

"Being here with these fancy people makes me

uncomfortable. I mean, look at how I'm dressed compared to that woman. Yeah, her outfit is sorta casual, but you know, on her way home, she's going to stop at the country club to say hi to Bipsy."

"Bipsy?" Sarah spluttered.

"I couldn't think of another pretentious name, but they all seem to go by silly nicknames, probably bestowed on them at birth by the Mayflower captain's ghost like it's a badge of honor." I shrugged.

"I told you not to wear your cargo shorts and *Spilling the Tea since 1773* T-shirt." Sarah's scrunched face screamed she'd been right, and I was most definitely in the wrong, but something told me she wasn't solely referring to my outfit choice. No matter what I did or where we went, I couldn't quite seem to fit in. Maybe I wasn't capable of it.

"I thought you meant because it was cloudy, not because there was a dress code for a kid's party." I tugged on the hem of my shirt to give me a better view of the cartoon depiction of the Boston Tea Party. "Besides, the shirt makes me smile. After the past two years, I've decided whenever I can, I'm doing things that give me happiness. This—" I jabbed my thumb into my chest, "makes me happy. Stepping in to teach a class I'm not responsible for, makes me unhappy, but I can't say no without looking like a jerk, which makes me doubly unhappy."

"You know what makes me happy?"

"Is this a trick question?" I took a step back out of

precaution, given her new habit of waving her arms around to get more steps. How many steps would she earn for biffing the back off my head?

"You seem scared." Sarah's smirk meant she enjoyed torturing me, but I was still stuck on her question, knowing full-well her happy thoughts probably didn't involve getting a bone saw from Santa. Sure, wishing for a bone saw might seem like a ticket onto the naughty list, but if Santa had to live under the same roof as my family, he'd probably understand my needs.

"I hate when you trick me," I mumbled.

"Don't make it so easy then."

"How did I do that?" I replayed the conversation in my head, seriously unable to pinpoint where I'd gone wrong. "Uh—?"

"It makes me happy when you listen to me," Sarah said with a slight pout. "I even set out clothes for you to wear today, you know."

"You did?"

"Yes. When you were in the shower."

"Oh. I thought those items were laundry. They looked like work clothes. I'm not working today. As you pointed out earlier, it's Saturday." Didn't she realize mixed messages—like don't work today because it's a weekend, but wear work clothes even though you're not working—would do my brain in?

"It's safe to say your brain is definitely on weekend mode."

"Hey!" I crossed my arms, obscuring the picture on my T-shirt. "I work hard all week."

Sarah leveled her dark chocolate eyes on mine. "While I sit at home all week eating bonbons?"

"Shittake." My head spun with how rapidly the conversation had taken a turn. "How did I get here?"

"You seem to think you aren't mean enough." Sarah crossed her arms, mimicking my stance. "I could always get a job, and you can stay home and raise our four kids."

To be totally honest, that sounded really, really hard. I'm sure my expression busted my true thoughts.

Sarah burst into laughter. "Yeah, that's what I thought. Now, if you'll excuse me, I need to say hi to Shrimpy over there."

"You made that up, didn't you?"

"You'll never know." Sarah sashayed across the playground, twisting her hips in that way of hers that could connect to a certain part of my body instantly, a part that should most definitely not jump to life at a kid's party.

"Mother fucker," I mumbled, looking anywhere but at Sarah while I waited for my temperature to go down. "What's that going to cost me?"

There was a chuckle behind me, and I spun around so fast I nearly wiped out again. I spied a woman roughly my age, one who was not wearing any diamonds. That fact put me at ease, at least somewhat.

"Sorry about my potty mouth. I wasn't calling my

spouse a mother fucker, just to be clear. Or anyone, really. I mean, no one here." My eyes scanned the children running amok, relieved no one seemed to be paying me any attention, aside from the woman who was studying me like I was a science experiment about to go *kablam*.

"You have more restraint than I do, then." The woman took a sip from her travel coffee cup. "I had too much fun on my mommy night out, and now the universe is punishing me with the worst hangover. I'm Tracy." She stuck her elbow out for a bump, which I clumsily met, still not handling this new human exchange that had taken the place of handshakes ever since the pandemic. I'd always been fond of squeezing the other person's hand to let them know I was in charge, but with an elbow bump, would too much force result in getting arrested for assault?

The woman seemed to be waiting for something. Belatedly, it hit me.

"L-Lizzie," I rushed to say, causing me to mess up my own name. "Sorry about my outfit."

This made Tracy outright laugh. "What's wrong with it?"

"Well…" I shifted on my feet. "I look nothing like anyone else here."

"Why do you think I came over?" she asked. "You seem to be normal."

If this chick thought I was normal, she was about to be sorely disappointed. As if needing to dispel her perception, I blurted, "I recently discovered I'm autistic. For real. Not self-diagnosed but legitimately confirmed by the powers that be last week."

"Cool." She spoke as if she believed that being autistic was indeed cool.

I decided if I had to befriend one of the moms so Sarah would get off my back, Tracy was my first choice. Let's face it; she was probably my only choice out of all the specimens on display.

"I've always wanted to be artistic," Tracy added with a smile.

Mother fucker.

CHAPTER TWO

A FLASH OF HORROR CROSSED TRACY'S FACE.

"I'm so sorry. I don't know you, and here I am making a stupid joke… er, not a *stupid* joke. It's the joke my son always makes. He's autistic, you see, but he likes to say he's *artistic*." The woman's face had turned beet red, and she hid behind her hands, looking like she wished she could disappear.

"Thank goodness." Realizing my own error, I frantically waved a hand in the air. "Not thank goodness he's autistic, although there's nothing wrong with that. It's just I thought you were nice, and I don't have many, or any, friends among the moms. Usually, it's my wife who makes friends. Speaking of," I paused, not sure if I should be grateful or mortified as Sarah approached, "Tracy, this is my wife, Sarah."

Sarah bumped elbows with Tracy, not looking the

least bit foolish as she did it. Why was everything so much easier for my wife?

"Tracy's son is autistic," I felt almost required to add as soon as the greetings were out of the way.

"Oh." Sarah bobbed her head in that nonchalant way she had, as if I'd said something totally normal, like the sun is yellow. But, Tracy's son was autistic, so didn't that make me saying it every bit as normal as commenting on anything else?

"Is it normal to be autistic?" I blurted.

This time, Sarah slanted her head, a smile spreading across her face. "It is in our family, with you and Fred."

"Fred's autistic!" Tracy's face brightened like a rainbow after a downpour, and then she spoke behind her hand. "I knew there was a reason I liked your family best."

"We should start a club or something. Call it the A-team." I laughed at my own joke, not feeling nearly as silly as I probably should have. It was like I'd wandered into a weird little bubble where the world made more sense. That hardly ever happened outside my own home, and even then, the experience was rare.

"A-team. That's adorable." Something caught Tracy's attention in the distance, and her expression darkened. "Oh shoot. My husband's here early. Gotta run."

She practically did run across the lawn, gathering her son like a superhero, before joining a stern looking man who was a dead ringer for a creepy priest in a horror flick, minus the collar.

"That's too bad," I commented, unable to keep my opinion to myself.

"What?" Sarah asked, either not sharing my first impression of Tracy's husband or doing a much better job of hiding her reaction. "Her son missing the surprise?"

"No." I frowned, belatedly processing her words. "Wait. What's the surprise?"

"I think for your birthday this year, I'm going to buy you a dictionary."

"I already have one," I was quick to remind her, only realizing after the words were out of my mouth what she'd really been trying to say. "Oh, that was a joke about not knowing the definition of the word surprise."

"By Jove, you're whip smart today!" Sarah squeezed my arm. "Now tell me what's too bad about Tracy?"

"Oh, you did catch that part," I replied. "I was hoping she was on our team."

"The A-team?" Sarah asked with a grin.

"No, the lesbian one."

"You know, you're allowed to have friends who aren't lesbians." Sarah swung an arm around my neck. "We can be friends with everyone."

"But I don't *like* everyone," I argued. Even as I said it, I fought the urge to shake off Sarah's arm, knowing it was meant to be a loving gesture but feeling like I

15

was being strangled by an octopus. "I find the more I have in common with people, the easier it is. I mean, Tracy didn't look like the type who'd enjoy discussing Hitler."

"That's the majority of the population, Lizzie."

"I know, which is why having the gay thing in common makes it easier. Besides, I'm tired of grumpy men. Did you get a load of her husband? Men like that have been taking up so much oxygen lately. Especially the bitter ones." It didn't help that a former male colleague of mine had tried to sabotage my career out of spite since I got a job over him. He'd been the type with the right last name and lineage for success, minus having a brain and ambition, but it didn't seem to register with him that he didn't get the job because of those qualities. Nope. It was easier to paint a target on me, the uppity lesbian who didn't deserve to have a job that was rightfully his. "How do people deal with grumpy spouses?"

"A lot of wine." Sarah sipped her drink, which I knew wasn't wine. Unless one of the snooty moms snuck some into the party.

"Am I as bad as that dude?" I hooked my thumb to the retreating back of Tracy and her family.

"Hard to say," Sarah said in her most reasonable tone. "I only saw him for a brief second and never got a chance to speak to him. But considering you're upset that you aren't mean enough, I would think you'd wear the label of grumpy spouse like a badge of honor."

"Whatever." As Sarah's arm shifted, I took the opportunity to make my escape. "I hope I'm wrong about that guy because Tracy seemed nice enough to pursue."

"Pursue?" Sarah burst into a loud guffaw. "Are you trying to make me jealous or something?"

I blinked, bewildered. "How in the world did you land on that?"

"You really don't know, do you?" That only made Sarah laugh harder, though I figured it was a common enough occurrence, she should have been immune to it by now. "Not to ruffle your feathers, dear, but from where I was standing, it *did* look a little like she was flirting with you."

"No, she wasn't. No one flirts with me. Hold on a second, missy." It took a few beats for some puzzle pieces to drop into place. "Did you come over here to mark your territory?"

If that were the case, I wasn't sure how to take the news. Happy? Annoyed? Fifty shades in between?

"Do I have to mark territory?" Sarah playfully crossed her arms, deepening the crease of her cleavage. I loved the fact that she wore a V-neck shirt that gave me more than a glimpse of the goods. She glanced down with faux innocence. "My secret weapon."

"Your boobs?"

Sarah winked, sending a fresh round of not-suitable-for-public sensations coursing through me. "This trick always works with you. Every. Damn. Time."

"Maybe that's what I want you to think," I protested, knowing I was full of it.

Her eyes narrowed. "Is that right?"

I raised my hands in the air. "Don't shoot."

Again, she laughed, and even after all of these years, the sound tickled my ears delightfully.

"Do I get to see more of them later?" I asked, holding my breath.

"If you play your cards right."

"Fu-fudge." I snapped my fingers as my face scrunched in disappointment. "You know I'm much better at messing up."

"True, but you seem to do okay for someone who's adorably clueless."

I stuck my tongue out at her for the second time that morning.

"Don't strain that. I'm counting on it being in fine form later tonight." She winked again and then slinked across the playground to a group of moms. It should be illegal for someone, even if that someone *was* my wife, to turn me on at a children's birthday party as much as she had. Fortunately, I restrained myself from shouting this sentiment across the sand. Even I knew that wouldn't go over well. Particularly with this crowd. I'd seen cardboard boxes with more personality.

This hadn't been part of my calculation when I

accepted a teaching job at the prestigious Wellesley College in Massachusetts. I'd had no frame of reference for the academic world outside of Colorado, having both gone to school and taught there. Here I had naively thought academics were stuck up in Fort Collins. Needless to say, I was completely unprepared for the rarified environment of the ivy elites.

It wasn't like I was some poor kid from the wrong side of the tracks, either. My father was wealthy. I had a trust fund, for heaven's sake. My mom, when she was still alive, had been the snobby country club sort. All of this, though, was in Denver, a kiddie pool by comparison to my new shark-eat-shark environment.

It wasn't simply my work colleagues who could be counted on to slip the name of their alma mater into any conversation, no matter how unrelated. I half expected that even at a dinner party the hosts would have special salt and pepper shakers just so they could say, "Excuse me, but could you pass the Yale salt, please?"

The professors were bad enough, but the parents in this town were cutthroat. It wasn't only about where they went to school, either. These people would compete over everything while trying to make it seem like they were above it all. It went beyond the brand of cars or the size of diamonds. There was a local preschool where a kid had to have had grandparents who'd attended the school as children to have a shot at getting in.

I'd found all this out the hard way, believe me. I didn't rub elbows that well with these old-money types. Yet, Sarah wanted us to get along for the sake of our children.

Which was why she had dragged me to this party, to force me to interact. So far, I'd talked to Tracy. For me that was going above and beyond both my parental and spousal duties for the day.

Sadly, Sarah did not share my assessment. Even now, she was waving me over to where she was speaking to a woman who, from the look of her, had to be the queen bee of all the moms.

Ugh. I didn't have a great experience with a Colorado queen bee of a mom group, but I suspected that was going to pale in comparison to what was in store for me now.

I took hesitant steps across the yard, wishing I could divert to where someone—the birthday kid's dad, maybe—was cooking hot dogs on a state-of-the-art grill. There was something about the smell of hot dogs on a grill on a beautiful spring day. Add in children's laughter, including two of my kids, and I should have been the happiest person on the planet.

Yet as I approached the gaggle of women, I couldn't get it out of my head that I was walking a plank. One wrong move and I'd be mom shark food.

I hated my life right then.

CHAPTER THREE

"Lizzie," Sarah said in a tone that was warm but laced with warning in a frequency only I—and possibly dogs—could hear. "I'd like you to meet Ingrid, our host today."

"Lovely to meet you." I put my hand out but quickly corrected to an awkward elbow bump. "Nice place. What's behind the gate?" I jerked my head to the left. "Is it where you lock up the bad party guests?"

Ingrid forced a smile before correcting me. "That's the pool and koi pond. The pool isn't open yet, but if this nice weather continues, I may ask Winslow, our handyman, to get it ready for us. Pool season is usually so short. It'd be a shame to miss out on days like this."

"A true travesty like—"

Sarah jabbed an elbow into my side before I could say the holocaust or something. I hadn't decided on where I was going, so it was probably a good thing Sarah stopped me before something truly absurd came spilling out.

"Leonard, come meet Sarah and Elizabeth."

"Lizzie," I corrected Ingrid, who didn't notice.

I couldn't be bothered to go out of my way to get the woman to respect my preferred name, so I turned to see who this Leonard was. I was pleasantly surprised to see a man sporting pink cargo shorts and a T-shirt with the *I'm Just a Bill* cartoon from *Schoolhouse Rock!*

"I have that shirt!" I said with way more excitement than a grown woman was probably supposed to show over a nerdy cartoon T-shirt. Or so I'd had it explained to me in similar situations before.

"Cracker Barrel?" he asked.

"Yes!" I clapped my hands together. "I'm almost certain that's where I got it. That place is dangerous. Between the gift shop and their chicken and dumplings—"

"That's my fave, too," Leonard jumped in to say, rubbing his belly.

I decided right then and there I liked him. This made two people in one day I'd met and not instantly disliked, which might have been a personal best.

Someone motioned to get Ingrid's attention. "I need to get back to my hostess duties. Make sure to get something to eat before the next phase."

"Phase?" I boosted my eyebrows at Sarah and Leonard.

"Ingrid takes children's parties very seriously." Leonard's unruly eyebrows bunched.

"How did you two meet?" I was having a hard time reconciling that this down-to-earth man married the likes of Ingrid.

"It was traumatic, really, but I have zero actual memories from that day."

"How so? Was it in an ER or something?" I wondered if Ingrid was a doctor. I hadn't thought to ask.

"Sorta. She's my twin."

"Really? We have twins!" I was practically hopping up and down, much to Sarah's amusement. Either that, or was she relieved I was chatting with a party-goer, even if I was acting like a buffoon.

"Lunch?" Leonard rubbed his hands together, and the three of us filed into one of the food lines.

The twins already sat at a table, their plates piled high with junk food galore, chattering away with their friends.

"Those are our twins." I gestured to Fred and Ollie. Fred was clearly in heaven since hot dogs were among his approved foods. I'll admit I was relieved to see normal party fare and not fancy catering food, and I could hardly stop myself from salivating in anticipation of the adults being called to the table. "Who belongs to you?"

"No kids for me," Leonard said. "I'm just an uncle, but I feel like I have hundreds sometimes, seeing as how I'm a school principal."

"At Wellesley High?" Sarah's head was turned toward Leonard as she handed me a plate. Unlike the paper ones the children were using, these were a thicker plastic that did a convincing job of looking like china, right down to a silver line around the edge.

"No," Leonard replied, also taking a plate. "I'm at a local charter school. I guess you might call me a free spirit, but I'm not one for traditional educational models. I think kids need more space to grow into their true selves, not what their parents or society want them to be. I hate seeing that spark of possibility being snuffed out at such a young age."

I scoped out all the parents and kids at the party, not spotting much individuality on display. I couldn't help thinking Leonard was in the minority, and I wondered how many kids were actually enrolled in this special school of his.

"I feel *exactly* the same way." Sara's tone when discussing teaching philosophies with Leonard was surprisingly reminiscent of how I'd sounded when extolling the virtues of the Cracker Barrel restaurant and gift shop. "Before having kids, I taught high school English in Colorado, but I felt stifled by the administration, who cared more about test scores than teaching critical thinking skills. I didn't care a whit about test scores. I cared about students finding reading to be the most exciting gift in the world and being able to articulate why they liked or hated something."

"English?" Leonard's eyes lit up almost as much as they had over chicken and dumplings. "Oh, man. I wish you worked at our school. I'm actually freaking out right now."

"Why's that?" I asked, noting that he was awfully calm for someone who was freaking out. I wondered how he pulled that off. I'd never been able to manage it.

"Our AP English Lit teacher's pregnant," he explained as the food line inched forward. "She's not due until the end of June, right after the term ends, but she's just been ordered on bed rest. I'm down one English teacher for the rest of the semester, and there aren't any qualified subs on the list."

I frowned as we reached the first platter of food on the serving table. "Where are the hot dogs?"

"Those are for the kids," Sarah said in a warning whisper before turning her attention to Leonard. "What are you going to do?"

"I might end up teaching the class myself at the rate things are going." Leonard's brow crinkled, and though his teacher situation did sound distressing, I suspected it was more because he, too, had gotten a look at the contents of the adult lunch table.

"I don't want any of this stuff." I surveyed the platters of fancy food, my eyes wandering from broccoli, brussels sprouts, asparagus, squash, and cauliflower. Every main dish option was drowning in creamy sauces. The type that made me want to puke. "Has Ingrid ever met a vegetable she doesn't like?"

"She hasn't, but I have." Leonard cast a longing look at the hot dogs across the way, confirming my suspicion that we were one hundred percent on the same page.

I let out an anguished sigh, wishing I hadn't informed Sarah earlier that I was a full-fledged adult. How was I supposed to foresee that would mean going without lunch?

"You like those." Sarah pointed to the mashed potatoes. "And I see rolls."

I offered a silent pout in response, but Leonard's eyes twinkled with a sudden mischief that offered hope.

"I think all the kids have their plates. What do you think?" He motioned toward the hot dog table.

"For a principal, you're a bad influence." Sarah laughed, but she stopped short of arguing with Leonard's plan. This was a little out of character for her, but I didn't want to point that out, considering I was on the verge of getting real food instead of filling up on potatoes and bread. If I was going to put on weight, I'd rather do so by eating grilled hot dogs than consuming a bunch of starch.

I ducked out of the line before Sarah could change her mind.

After Leonard and I piled our plates high with dogs and chips, while Sarah put roasted asparagus and hummus on hers in a quantity that I could only assume was done to make a point, we found seats together at an empty table. Sarah began grilling Leonard about his charter school, and while I liked the man enough, I was way more interested in enjoying the char on my first hot dog to pay much attention to what they were saying. As a bonus, Sarah was so engrossed in the conversation, she didn't seem to notice when I went back to add more potato chips to my plate. It felt like it was *my* birthday party, and I wasn't going to waste a second of this indulgence.

But before I could demolish all the salty goodness, my eyes spied something that made me question my sanity even more than I usually did.

"Is that—?" I couldn't complete the sentence and resorted to pointing. Either it was a figment of my imagination and a sign I was finally due for a long stay at a facility with padded walls, or there was a man on the other side of the black wrought iron fence wearing a red costume with yellow piping, black tights, boots, and a silly hat like he traveled in time from King Arthur's court.

"A herald. Yes." Leonard wiped ketchup off his chin. "Ingy has a fondness for pageantry."

The herald blew a horn.

"Children! Time to come inside to get dressed." Ingrid clapped her hands together, rallying the kids from their junk food comas. I was amazed not one had puked yet. That always seemed to happen at every birthday party.

"Dressed for what? Jousting?" I asked Sarah in a loud whisper. I wondered if this was a sign it was time for me to grab Fred and Olivia and run for our lives.

Sarah shrugged, apparently able to let everything play out without the slightest flutter of panic in her heart. I wished I knew her secret. I hated not knowing what was going on. There were two words that never described me when put together: easy and going.

No one was going to make my kids joust. What was this? *The Hunger Games?*

"Should I follow them?" I started to get up, but Leonard shook his head and motioned for me to sit back down.

"I wouldn't interfere unless you want to get zapped by Ingy's whip. It's how I got this scar on my chin." He rubbed a jagged white line on his face I hadn't noticed before. "She doesn't like insubordination of any type."

He started to laugh, and Sarah joined in. Meanwhile, I lost my appetite. A true shame because I still had half of my second hot dog and a decent amount of chips left. I was truly starting to hate this Ingrid.

Soon enough, the kids started spilling back outside, in full princess or prince outfits that easily could have been sewn by an entire brigade of Walt Disney's magical mice.

"Oh, that's right," Leonard said with a nod. "The party favors. I'd forgotten she mentioned those."

"Favors, like the kids can take them home?" My jaw dropped as I estimated the price of each costume and multiplied it by the ungodly number of children attending the party. I remembered stuffing party favors for one of the kid's birthdays a while back. They'd included bubbles, Sponge Bob stamps, and silly finger traps. Not tailored Disney outfits.

Then my eyes landed on Fred and Ollie, and everything was right in the world again, making me laugh. Sarah followed my eyes, joining in.

"Fred makes a beautiful princess, and Olivia is the handsomest prince ever." I beamed at my free thinkers, snapping a photo on my phone.

All the parents followed the kids to the side of the house, which had been blocked off until now with pipe and drape barriers that could've been concealing a top-secret government project. The reason for the secrecy soon became apparent. There before our eyes was a perfect miniaturized replica of the Sleeping Beauty castle. This was not the usual bouncy house type, but one that could rival the one at Disneyland, despite it not being to scale.

It was more like a really large children's playhouse version but still substantial enough to puzzle me. How in the heck had they gotten it here? Had they used one of those trailers that can move half a house? Was it in two pieces and glued together? What must people have thought driving down the highway with a giant castle in the lane next to them?

I was so taken by the castle that I didn't see the snow-white pony until it neighed, causing me to jump. There were actors in costume, too, making the fantastical scene all the more believable, in a thoroughly fantastical way.

"I thought your tent birthday party was over the top, but this takes the cake." I whistled. "Is that a horse?"

"Unicorn," Sarah said, like it wasn't the craziest thing she'd ever seen.

"But it's not actually a unicorn, right?" I blinked rapidly, convinced my eyes were deceiving me. "Because I could have sworn unicorns were extinct."

Sarah gaped at me. "Please tell me you're kidding."

"I don't even know anymore. Is this a dream?" I put my arm out for her to pinch.

CHAPTER FOUR

"Why are you so annoying?" Olivia, our oldest child, crossed her arms in the middle of our kitchen, daring me to challenge or refute her.

"It's in my DNA, which means it's also in your DNA." I patted the top of her head, which still contained traces of glitter from the party the day before.

"Lizzie!" Sarah jumped in, glancing up from her phone. "Do not call one of our kids annoying?"

"I didn't! Not outright. Besides, I'm simply pointing out a scientific fact."

"To our *daughter*. And, Ollie, don't be mean."

"I wasn't," Ollie had the audacity to say.

"Don't talk back to me." Sarah crossed her arms, one hand still clutching her phone, it beeping to alert her there was a new message.

"See!" I pointed. "It runs in the family. You both have the same combative stance." Technically, we'd used my egg when undergoing IVF for the twins, but this particular scientific fact didn't help my argument. I pressed my lips together to keep it inside, practically causing me physical pain.

Sarah gave me a knowing look, grinning.

Was she enjoying the fact that I wanted to spill the beans about the egg situation? She could be evil sometimes. She had to know how hard it was for me.

As if reading my thoughts, Sarah said to me, "Lizzie, apologize to Ollie."

"For what?"

"Seriously, sometimes I wonder which one of you is actually the grown-up."

"Not it," Ollie and I said in unison, and then we high-fived.

Sarah blew a raspberry. "I'm not speaking to either of you."

It sounded lighthearted on the surface, but I knew my wife well enough by now to detect a seething anger that Sarah didn't want to let out in front of our daughter. After all these years, detecting was still as far as I could go. As for what was angering her, I had no clue. Not knowing what to do, I hunched down. "Olivia, you are not annoying. I'm sorry I implied it. Let's hug it out." I spread my arms, and she fell into the embrace.

"Love you, Mommy."

I squeezed her tighter, nuzzling my nose against her head. "Ditto, kiddo."

Olivia ran out of the house into the backyard where the rest of the family had gathered for our weekly Sunday night dinner. Given the predicted rain never arrived, we decided to grill.

"You okay?" I asked Sarah when she turned around to pull some plates from the cupboard.

"We need to talk."

My heart came to a screeching halt, lodging itself into my throat. Never have more terrifying words been uttered in the history of the universe than those four when said by one's spouse.

I swallowed down the hard lump. "Ollie and I were just teasing each other. We do it all the time."

"I know. Not about that. The adulting part."

"It's way too early to make Ollie behave like an adult. As someone who didn't have a great childhood, I want our kids to be that. Kids."

Sarah crossed her arms, giving me her best *don't be an idiot* look. "I'm talking about you."

"Me?" I placed a hand on my chest, and to be honest, I really hadn't seen that coming. "You don't think I adult well?"

"On some fronts. The bills are always paid on time. Early, even. You've always been employed." She stopped, and it wasn't a sudden stop, like when one of the kids interrupted her. No, instead she seemed to have run out of examples. This did not bode well for me.

"I'm the mother of four kids."

"Are you?" Sarah, head down, counted out forks to bring outside. Despite not always being the brightest at these things, I sensed I was lucky one of those forks wasn't currently lodged in my chest.

"What are you really saying?" This might not have been the wisest thing to ask, given I suspected the answer would sting, and Sarah seemed to be in a mood to really let me have it. But I had no idea why, and I needed to know.

"I'm tired of being the only full-time stay-at-home mom."

"You want me to trade places with you?" I scratched my head, dumbfounded. "How would that even work?"

"No, that's not what I'm saying. And as for how it would work, one word: chaos." She looked me straight in the eye. My belly tightened as I failed to detect a single trace of humor in the crinkles around her eyes.

"Geez, don't soften your opinion to avoid hurting my feelings."

Sarah let out a burst of warm breath. "You're brilliant on many levels, but managing a house with four kids isn't your strong suit. It's why I want to hire a nanny."

"A nanny? Why in the world do we need a nanny?"

"Because I want help around here." Sarah opened

her mouth, closed it, and then opened it again, the words coming out in a rush. "And because I want to go back to work."

"I thought the kids were your job."

Sarah held a handful of knives, and I was dead certain this time she wanted to drive all of them deep into my chest. Slowly, she set them onto the counter and then gripped the edges of the granite with both hands, speaking ever so slowly in her forced calm voice usually reserved for a child who'd stepped on her last nerve. "Lizzie. I've been at home for nearly six years. I miss being around adults."

"There are other adults here," I said quietly. "Some of them are even more adult than I am, probably."

"That's not the point. I miss having a job." Sarah's tone was imploring. "I have to get out of this house. I need to stimulate my mind. I love you. I love the kids. I love being a mom. But I need *more*."

My eyes fell to the knives, which were still too close to Sarah's hands. "What kind of job do you want?"

"Teaching."

"Don't you have to do a bunch of stuff with your teaching credential from Colorado? That could take a while."

She shook her head. "Actually, no. The requirements for substitute teaching aren't difficult at all. They're desperate after the pandemic."

It seemed there was a lot of desperation around

me, but I locked that thought inside, keeping a vigilant eye on the stack of weapons at Sarah's disposal, thanking the stars they weren't steak knives. How much damage could common dinnerware do? I didn't want to find out.

"Why do we need a nanny, though?" I pressed, going after the real sticking point in her proposal. "Yes, I teach full-time, but I'm only on campus a few days a week. I can be here when you're teaching. Not to mention, your mom is close, and now my dad and Helen are, too."

"Our parents are the kids' grandparents, not nannies."

"Okay, well, we can talk about getting a nanny after the summer." I loved putting off difficult conversations.

"We need to talk about it now."

"Why? The school year is almost over. No one's hiring for this year."

"Lenny just texted. He offered me a contract for the rest of this semester."

"Who the f-fork is Lenny?" Even after all these years, I still had to stop myself from using curse words on the off chance little ears were eavesdropping.

"Ingrid's brother. You remember. We met him yesterday."

"The one with the cartoon shirt?" My jaw slackened. I'd been betrayed by someone I'd been certain was a kindred spirit. This was why people were so overrated.

"Yes. He wants me to step in for the pregnant teacher who had to go on leave. You do remember that conversation, right? Or were you too busy being upset that you had to cover one person's class that you totally tuned out the part where he had to find a qualified English teacher with two days' notice?"

I vaguely remembered the conversation in question, so I nodded, not wanting to give Sarah the satisfaction of being right. "When would you start?"

"This week."

"But—I—how will this work?" I was truly at a loss, details spinning around like a jumble of puzzle pieces all turned in the wrong direction. Sarah hadn't worked a day outside the house since the kids were born. Now, all of a sudden, she had a job lined up, and it started right away? My brain didn't work that quickly about anything. It needed to percolate.

"That's what I've been telling you. We need help. Ingrid mentioned a friend who'd recently used an agency to find a nanny, and—"

"No way. No can do. Even if I said yes to a nanny, it's not like we can pick one in a day and feel safe about the choice. Unless Ingrid's friend knows the actual Mary Poppins." Sensing I jumped the gun on saying no, I joked, "Does she?" I started to hum "Supercalifragilisticexpialidocious."

That didn't soften Sarah's stance. In fact, I think her right eye started to twitch.

I opted for Plan B. "What if we split everything fifty-fifty when it comes to taking care of the kids and things around the home?"

"What things around the home?"

"Uh…cooking, cleaning. You know, things."

"I'm well aware of the things involved. Clearly, you are not."

Sarah had me there, and I shrugged helplessly. Which was why she'd put me on the spot. I'd walked right into a Sarah trap, not for the first time and probably not for the last.

She glared at me before sweeping up the tray with all the supplies she'd gathered during our chat—or lecture was more the word for it—and going to the backyard. I stood in the kitchen trying to come up with a rebuttal that didn't make me sound like a total jerk.

Sadly, I think that boat had left the shore, and now I was stranded, surrounded by hungry sharks in the water in the form of Rose, Sarah's mom, Helen, my dad's wife, and Maddie, our best friend who loved to point out all my faults.

Perhaps it was best to fake a heart attack or something.

Willow, Maddie's girlfriend and my podcast partner, came into the kitchen. "Sarah says you're hiding, and I should bring you outside, kicking and screaming. Her words, not mine."

"I guess the heart attack option is off the table."

"What?"

"Nothing. Do we need anything else?"

"I'm pretty sure Sarah's taken care of all the details."

"Yeah. She does that." I squeezed my eyes shut as it sank in that she wasn't going to be doing that anymore. "And she makes it all look so effortless. How do I compete with that?"

"Why would you want to compete with Sarah?"

I appreciated Willow not laughing and instead asking the question honestly, giving me the opportunity to open up or not. I probably should have taken her up on it, but I hadn't quite processed everything yet, so I simply shrugged and rowed out, so to speak, to face the sharks.

Helen, my dad's second wife, came over and put her arm around my waist. "I didn't think you were going to join us."

"I wasn't sure if I was welcome," I muttered.

She scrunched her eyebrows, and Sarah, who was close enough to hear, let out an angry sigh.

Helen let it go, while Rose dug her eyes into mine. I tried to determine if she knew the source of Sarah's anger or if she was simply siding with Sarah out of motherly duty.

I glanced toward our kids. They were playing soccer on the lawn, or rather using the soccer ball as a prop for what may have been a play of some type.

Each of the four kids were speaking rapidly, even Demi. That warmed my heart. We'd adopted Demi after her father, my brother, went to prison for financial shenanigans, and it took time for her to settle into our rambunctious house. Now she was bossing Calvin, our youngest son, around, bringing a grin to my face.

Sarah met my eye and smiled as well, meaning I wasn't completely in the doghouse, but her stiff shoulders screamed I still had some work to do to get back into her good graces. Or even into the same zip code.

"You excited for Cal and Demi to go to preschool this fall?" Maddie asked, which seemed like an odd question. I was a college professor. Of course, I supported school. Was this Maddie's way of letting me know she'd already heard about the dust-up over Sarah substitute teaching? I wouldn't be surprised if she'd known what was coming before I did. I was usually the last to know anything.

"We've been working on the alphabet and counting," I foolishly said as if that was all that mattered. Was it? What else was there about preschool?

"They'll get to make friends," Sarah added. "They're important."

Friends. I should've guessed.

"So you keep telling me." I opened the blue cooler and fished in the ice for a Coke Zero.

"It's important for kids to have friends," Sarah said as if restating it would drill it through my thick skull.

My eyes returned to the kids. Freddie now wore an eye patch and was wielding a plastic sword.

"Not just siblings." Sarah cut me off before I had a chance to say the line I'd always stuck to.

Growing up, I'd had a brother who tortured me. I would have killed to have three siblings with whom I could play. For me, that achievement in our family was one of my proudest accomplishments.

"The twins have a playdate at the Dowds this Saturday. Lizzie, why don't you take them to see how much they love it and to start our new fifty-fifty deal? Maybe you'll make friends as well. You need some." Sarah left to supervise Troy and my father at the grill.

"Okey dokey, Smokey," I called out to her. How hard could it be to take kids to a playdate? "Do I just drop them off?"

Sarah shot me a look that warned I was totally off base, and my spirits fizzled. Looked like there was more to the playdate than I thought.

"Have you met that mom group?" Maddie asked, confirming my suspicions that this was going to be a social gathering for me as well as the kids.

Damn.

"Uh…" All the different mom groups were the same in my book. Full of themselves, judgmental, and they'd stab themselves in the back just to get a leg up.

"They're fun. I was there two weekends ago, and oh man, I woke up with a killer headache the next day."

Great. Just what I needed. A loud playdate. I'd grown accustomed to the rowdiness of my own children, but I loved them. I didn't particularly enjoy other people's kids until they reached college age.

Not that I could say that given the earlier conversation, so I simply said, "Looking forward to it," before slamming half of my drink, praying for the caffeine to power me through the family dinner without bursting into tears or screaming. Perhaps both.

CHAPTER FIVE

"We have a problem." Sarah stood in the kitchen, an iced coffee in her hand. The drink was in a travel tumbler, and she was wearing nice trousers and a blouse, or what I used to call her "teacher" clothes. Somewhere in the back of my mind, a red flag began to wave.

"Good morning. Isn't it a lovely spring day? The birds are singing. There's no humidity. The kids and I just returned from an educational walk." I kissed her cheek before flipping on the electric kettle to make a fresh cup of tea. In other words, I did what I always do when presented with a red flag. I ignored it.

"Where are the kids?" Sarah asked with a frown, a tense line forming between her brows.

"There was a friendly stranger with a van who offered to take them to the candy shop. Who was I to say no?" I wheeled about to see her laugh.

Sarah, who usually got my sense of humor, did not laugh. Instead, she stared daggers at me. "I'm not in the mood."

"For strangers? Or candy?" Because if there's one thing that can revive a joke that fell flat the first time, it's telling it twice.

"I forgot about my appointment with Lou, which I'll obviously have to cancel. This will mean it's been scheduled and then rescheduled three times."

I touched my tongue to my lower lip as I thought. "Lou's the contractor, right? For the basement project?"

"Yes."

I put my hand up, totally deserving a high five for remembering that detail. Sarah left me hanging. "Do you normally get this dressed up for a contractor?"

"Are you even listening to me?"

I swallowed hard. This usually meant I hadn't been and that I'd better start, or else there would be hell to pay. "Why do you have to cancel?"

In my opinion, Sarah looked more than presentable for a meeting with a contractor. What was the big deal?

"I need to leave the house in five minutes, or I'll be late."

Oh.

"Wait." I swallowed again. "You have plans this morning?"

"I told you yesterday. I start teaching today." She motioned to her outfit like that should have clued me in. Okay, yes. They were her teacher clothes, but that hadn't made the necessary connection in my noggin, and frankly, I was still struggling. She had to be mistaken.

"It's a holiday," I argued.

Sarah arched a brow. "What holiday?"

I threw my hands in the air. "I don't know. The kids don't have school, so I assumed it was a holiday kids get but not college professors."

"No. It's an in-service day for the elementary school. There's an environmental disaster specialist coming to prep teachers for all sorts of emergency situations that could arise in the event of extreme weather. After that, they'll be running an active shooter simulation. It's all in the weekly email you never read."

"Is that what you're doing today?" Honestly, that seemed strange because I didn't think substitutes had to sit in on those kinds of meetings. Not that any teacher should have to do half the things expected of them these days. Climate disaster training? Active shooter drills?

"No. I'm teaching. The charter school doesn't have teacher training today."

The meaning of Sarah's words finally hit me, and I staggered back a step. "Umm... Are you telling me we're sending our kids to a school that's preparing for shootings? Floods? Tornadoes? Zombies?"

Ignoring my distress, Sarah typed rapidly on her phone. "We're never going to get the basement done at this rate."

"Because of zombies?"

Her eyes became little more than dark slits. "Are you intentionally trying to annoy me?"

I really wasn't, but given the creases in her forehead, there was no amount of explaining I could do to make her believe me. Sometimes, the woman could be completely unreasonable.

The basement. She was upset about not being able to meet Lou. *Come on, Lizzie. Get into the game.*

"What time is the meeting with Lou?" I asked. "If it's early enough in the day, I can do that before I head to campus."

"You don't go to campus on Mondays."

"I have to fill in today. Remember? Dead brother."

"Isn't it a night class?"

"No. It's at one in the afternoon." I could've made a snide comment about who wasn't listening now, but I refrained. I deserved a goddamn medal.

Sarah's face drained. "I won't be home until after four-thirty."

"It looks like they'll need a sub for their sub," I joked. Only, I wasn't exactly joking. Was it such a surprise the teaching thing wasn't working out, given how little time there had been to plan? We could always try again in the fall. Or later. Like maybe when the kids were all in college.

"That's not going to happen," Sarah said in the same stern tone she used on the kids when they were naughty. "I agreed. I can't back out now."

"But I have a job," I spluttered. "A real job. You can't expect me to fill in here at the last second."

"What happened to fifty-fifty?" Sarah steadied her eyes on me, preparing for battle.

"That was before I knew it was starting today. I wasn't prepared for today. I thought wearing them out on a walk before going to campus would be helpful, but I didn't know…" I blinked rapidly, mesmerized by the flashes of light in front of my eyes. "What am I supposed to do with four kids all day when I have a stack of research papers to grade and a class to babysit? Plus, I still have to write my podcast script for tonight's recording." I was starting to sweat about all the things that needed to be done, which was a pretty normal workload, aside from the four kids part.

This might have been the absolute worst thing to say to Sarah, especially before she'd finished her first iced coffee. I'd been informed in the past, if she killed me before getting the right amount of caffeine into her bloodstream, no jury would convict her. Especially if all the members of the jury were stay-at-home moms.

"What time is the meeting with the contractor?" If I got her back on that, she might have forgotten the *real job* dig.

"Ten."

"I can handle that. And, I'll call my dad to see if he can help out."

"With the contractor?" Sarah snapped her fingers. "Why didn't I think of that?"

"I meant this afternoon with the kids when I have to pop over to campus."

"Do you really think you can handle the contractor on your own? You've said yourself a million times you're not great with people or numbers. This will involve both of those things." She spoke in her soft tone, the one that annoyed me every single time because it implied that I absolutely should not get upset.

"Is the contractor a mean mom?"

"I doubt it. His name's Lou. I'm guessing he's a big hairy guy with a butt crack problem."

"Why are we hiring Mr. Butt Crack?" I tried shaking off the image. Would the crack also be hairy? I did not want an answer to that question.

"It's just a meeting to see if we want to hire him, although so far, he's the only one who's responded to my emails and texts. It's a nightmare hiring people these days."

"I wish we could hire a woman. Do you know most of history is filled with men? I've been trying to find a significant birth or death every day of a woman to share the facts with the kids, and most of the women mentioned are actors." I held up my hand, even though Sarah didn't look like she was about to interject or was even listening. "While there's nothing wrong with acting as a profession, why do we only know about the great men in every other possible field in history?"

"I'm sorry, but are you really just figuring this out?" She stared at me like I'd had rocks in my head instead of a brain.

"Yes and no. Ever since we had daughters, I've been noticing a lot of things. Most kid books have boys. More of the toys are for boys. It's like society and the world has decided girls don't matter. I want to change that, and I want Freddie and Calvin to be feminists. Hence why I've been trying to find more women in history to talk about on our morning walks." I plopped a tea bag into my mug, adding a small splash of honey, and then a little more when Sarah turned her back. "You should join us on the walks. Today we learned about—"

"Lizzie, I would rather your dad or Helen be here for the contractor. Maddie can't. I already asked her."

"Because you don't trust me, which is insulting, frankly. Here I am, adulting, which you wanted me to do more of. You can't pick and choose what I can adult."

"Don't try using guilt on me."

"It's perfectly reasonable, given the thread of this conversation. Also, I'm quite capable of meeting with a contractor, thank you very much." I tossed a second tea bag into my mug, because I was going to need all the help I could get today. "While I don't like people much, I do have to interact with them all the dang time. Do you think meeting a contractor is harder than a departmental meeting? Let me tell you the answer is no. Historians are long-winded, full of themselves, and contentious."

"No. Really?" She feigned being knocked over with a feather.

"Just for that, you can go to work all day for your punishment. Find out the grass isn't greener on the other side. Work is hard!"

"I'm going to pretend you didn't say that." She let out an angry huff of air. "Seriously, where are the kids?"

"In the backyard with Maddie and Willow. You left me a note to have the kids back in time for a photo shoot with Maddie. Is that the new thing? Photo shoots? First at the party. Now here. It's like everyone wants their kids to become Instagram influencers." There was a lot more I could have said on this topic, but as I sucked in a breath to continue, Sarah cut me off.

"That's right! I forgot. It's part of the twin's art project. Maddie's helping them."

"Luckily, I didn't forget about the shoot." Although I had no memory of it being part of a homework assignment. Still, I was proud of myself for not forgetting to be back in time for it, even if I didn't know why.

"It's killing you, isn't it? Not rubbing it in my face that you remembered something I didn't?"

"You have no idea."

"I have some idea considering you look like you're constipated. Are you sure you can handle the contractor?"

"One hundred percent. Basically, I need to get a sense if he can be trusted. I'm good at figuring out if people are full of shit."

Sarah was about to say something but stopped herself. "Okay. I better get on the road."

"Have fun."

"Is that all you have to say to me?"

I blinked.

"It's my first day back in the classroom."

"Right. No kicking, biting, hitting, screaming, or crying." I playfully tapped the side of my cheek. "I think that's all of them."

"I'm the teacher."

"I know. A hot teacher." I moved in for a kiss. "Good luck, today."

"You, too."

"You have no idea how adulty I can be when given the chance."

"Actually, I do. That's what has me worried." She glanced at the time again, heaved a resigned sigh, waved goodbye, and left in a rush.

When alone in the kitchen, I glanced down at Gandhi, our yorkie who was worn out from the walk and sprawled out on the cool floor, panting. "I don't get women."

He raised his head ever so slightly to give me a look that screamed, "No shit, Sherlock."

CHAPTER SIX

I ANSWERED THE FRONT DOOR, EXPECTING TO lock eyes on Mr. Butt Crack. It was a meeting I wasn't looking forward to, but after making such a stink about how capable I was, I'd backed myself into a corner. A specialty of mine.

Instead of the big, hairy man I had pictured, a petite woman stood on my front doorstep. She wore cargo pants, and all the pockets were crammed with what seemed like useful things. She also wore a tight-fitting shirt, equally admirable in its own way.

"Um, is this the Petrie residence?"

Stop gawking, Lizzie!

"Oh, sorry. I was expecting someone else. How can I help you? Do you need directions?"

"Actually, I think I'm the person you're expecting. The name's Louise, but everyone calls me Lou."

"You're a woman!" I exclaimed with what was

probably a tad too much excitement. Considering the extra seconds, I'd spent staring at her shirt, I didn't want Lou to get the wrong idea. It was just that I could handle a female contractor easy-peasy, at least compared to how I would do with a hairy guy. The day was looking up.

"Why don't people look at my bio on my website before they waste my time?" Lou muttered as she started to walk away.

"Don't go!" I called out, panicking that I might have managed to screw this up already. "That probably came out wrong. The thing is, this morning, I told my wife I wished we could hire a woman, and not a man with an ugly butt crack."

Lou turned around, and by the expression on her face, she hadn't decided if I was for real or not. I couldn't blame her. First impressions—good ones, at least—weren't in my wheelhouse. I was starting to see why Sarah didn't trust me with this meeting.

"No, really. I'm so over men in all aspects of life. That came out wrong, and it's not entirely true. I mean, there's not much I can do about the fact that I have a father and brothers. It's not like I can kill them or anything." *Shut up, Lizzie.* "I'm Lizzie, by the way. Lizzie Petrie, not Borden. You're safe."

Lou took my extended hand with trepidation, and I was pretty sure it wasn't because of COVID concerns, even though I had yet again forgotten the whole elbow bump thing.

"Let me show you the basement." I heard what I said the second the words left my mouth. "I swear. I'm not a serial killer or anything. This has been a morning. My wife usually handles these meetings. But she left me all alone with four kids for the entire day, and I'm like—" I did my best frazzled scream by way of illustration. "Do you want to come back when Sarah's here?"

My shoulders sagged. I was every bit as bad at this as Sarah had no doubt expected me to be.

"It's fine. I'll keep ahold of my hammer." It hung on her belt, and up until now, I'd had no idea how sexy that could be. In the abstract. It wasn't like I was going to start hitting on the woman. I'd scared her enough. Also, that hammer should have been a huge effing clue that she was the contractor. Now, I felt like a total idiot.

Back to the tool belt, though. Maybe I should buy Sarah one. It wasn't like our bedroom activities had been all that great lately. One of us was usually too tired or upset over something. Life, lately, seemed too stressful with me worrying about everything under the sun and Sarah getting annoyed with me stressing about things I couldn't control.

A tool belt, though. That could spice things up. Without the hammer, obviously. I wasn't about to provide Sarah with the means and opportunity to put an end to me. I already supplied plenty of motive.

As Lou and I descended the stairs, I wanted to see

if she was now holding the hammer in head-whacking range but was too fearful to look over my shoulder. If she was, the last thing I wanted was to startle her, possibly resulting in my own decapitation. How could I save this appointment and prove to Sarah I wasn't entirely inept?

Offer twice Lou's asking price and beg her to take the job?

No. Sarah would kill me.

We reached the partially finished basement, and I tried to calmly explain our vision about creating an apartment for Maddie and Willow.

After taking a spin through the basement, Lou tapped her pen against a clipboard. "This won't take too much work, really."

"To make an apartment and carve out a small podcast studio?" I didn't want to outright call her a liar, but to me, it seemed like a monumental task. However, I wasn't the DIY type, mostly because everyone, including me, didn't trust me around power tools.

"Yep. I'm picturing it." She rapped her pen on the side of her head. "Is it your podcast or your wife's?"

"Mine. With Willow. Who'll be living in the apartment."

"What's it about?" Lou jotted some numbers down on her paper.

"History. We're both historians." I mumbled most of this sentence, expecting her eyes to glaze over.

"That's cool. What's it called?" She had her phone out, tapping on her podcast app.

I told her.

"Hold the phone." She slowly raised her eyes to mine. "You're Lizzie!"

"Yes." I thought that introducing myself in the beginning would have cleared that up, but it wasn't like I could call her out on that considering my poor performance from the start.

"Oh my goodness. It's all finally clicking in my head. And, Willow. Oh my God!"

"You… you've heard of us?"

"Heard of you? I'm a huge fan." From the look of excitement on Lou's face, I actually believed her and was completely gobsmacked by the revelation. We had fans? "I wouldn't miss an episode. I love the banter between you two. Not only do I learn fascinating tidbits, but it's nice to know true friendships still exist in this world of divisiveness."

"We didn't start out that way. At first, I couldn't stand her." I wished I hadn't said this. "I mean it was the beginning of lockdown, and she showed up out of the blue to live with us. I don't handle change, and that was a whoop-ass dose of change."

"Yeah, but now you two get along. I think that's even cooler." Lou took out a tape measure. "Knowing who you are, though, I'm surprised you're not asking about building a bunker. I've heard you refer to yourself as a bunker type minus the bunker." She laughed, while happily jotting numbers on her pad.

My brain kicked into action, my pulse quickening. "Are you telling me you know how to build bunkers? Like, would that sort of thing be possible?"

"You should see what people do. Anything is possible." She waggled her eyebrows. "Well, I think I have everything I need to write up the quote. Should I email it to you or Sarah?"

"Hold on a second. Can we circle back to the bunker idea?" I made a circle with my fingers like Lou needed an example. "How would that work exactly? I used to joke I wanted to build a moat around my house, filled with alligators and crocodiles to keep my family away, but they moved to Massachusetts to be closer to me." I offered a *what can you do* shrug. "A bunker seems more prudent."

Lou blinked, unsure how to react, or so it looked to me. It was a reaction many people had around me.

"With the war in Ukraine, climate change, and all the fucking crazies… are bunkers really a thing? Would it be waterproof, airtight, and stop the zombie apocalypse?" My thoughts returned to the training at my kids' school. Were they going to build a bunker as well? Should we all get them?

"Yeah, bunkers exist. I mean, it's mostly for the super-rich or doomsday fanatics, but they're definitely a thing. In fact, just the other day, I saw an article on the bunkers of the rich and famous. They're nice."

"Can you email me the article?"

"Sure, but it might be quicker to google it."

"Brilliant." I did as she suggested. "Wow. Look at this one with the swimming pool." I turned my phone for her to see.

She whistled her appreciation.

"This one has a *view* of Tower Bridge in London." I made quote marks with one hand when speaking the word *view* since I was fairly sure it wasn't real. "I wonder if they can change it to different locations each day. That would be awesome. Too bad Sarah won't go for this. Not after all the arguments we've had about my desire to move to Mars."

Lou laughed, more than likely thinking I was kidding, because what couple argued about something that wasn't a possibility? Not yet at least, because I firmly believed it was going to happen. Big surprise, Sarah was in the naysayer camp. She could be so short-sighted sometimes it was as if she liked stabbing me in the heart with her negativity when all I was trying to do was protect my family.

"So, obviously these places are much larger and are designed to allow for this luxury. But what about here? Could you tunnel a simple bunker for me, just in case?"

"Tunnel. That's funny." She laughed but stopped. "You're serious? I mean, it sounds like you truly want me to draw up plans for a bunker."

"It doesn't hurt. I'll pay you for your time even if I

—we, that is—decide against it." Naturally, Sarah would need to be in on this planning. Unless… maybe she didn't need to know. She'd left me in charge of the meeting, which meant the final say was technically up to me. Right?

Lou bobbed her head. "I should tell you, I haven't personally built a bunker before."

"No, I imagine not. And, like I said, I just want to know if it's possible. To help me sleep better at night, which isn't a lot, lately. This thing—never turns off." I held a hand to the side of my head, accidentally making a finger gun. *Great, Lizzie. Scare the poor contractor with all your lunatic bunker talk after all the crazy babble from earlier.*

But, as soon as the word bunker entered my head, I knew I wouldn't be able to let it go. It was a trait that drove Sarah bonkers. I started to laugh. Bonkers over a bunker. I kinda wanted to tell her that part because it might put her in a good mood. Then again, she might lock me up and throw away the key. No, it was better to keep this to myself. For now.

CHAPTER SEVEN

I escorted Lou to the door and gave her my email to send me all the details. Once the door shut, I felt pretty good overall. I was getting a quote, which was what Sarah wanted. Plus, I knew Rose would be over any minute to watch the kiddos. That meant I could give one lecture at the college and then rush back. This whole fifty-fifty parenting thing was falling into place.

I waved to Willow as she breezed past me toward the door. She'd been keeping an eye on the kids during my meeting, but now she was on her way to the community college. Maddie had left right before Lou arrived for an appointment in Boston, which meant until Rose came over, I was all alone with the kids.

No problem. I had it all under control.

Even as I was thinking this, my phone rang, which

was unusual. Only two people I knew called me: Rose and my dad.

Sure enough, it was Rose.

"Excited to have time with the kids?" I asked, not bright enough to sense any impending doom.

"I'm sorry, Lizzie. But I have to cancel," Rose said, bringing my perfect plan tumbling down around me like a house of cards.

"What? Why?" All four kids ran by, screaming. I plugged my free ear with a finger.

"I sneezed," Rose answered, though I wasn't certain at first that I'd heard her right.

"Sneezed? Like achoo?"

"Yes. I just can't risk coming over unless I take a COVID test, but we're out."

Probably because every time the woman sneezed, she tested herself. "I'm sure it's fine, Rose. I mean, everyone sneezes sometimes. It's spring."

"Even so, I'd never forgive myself if I got the kids sick."

I wanted to cry, but that wasn't an option. "I'll call Helen to see if she can come over."

"She's with your dad," Rose reminded me. "He's having his colonoscopy today."

"Right." Well, that bit me in the ass, didn't it? "Okey dokey, Smokey. I'll figure things out."

We ended the call, and I checked the time. I had one hour and fifty-five minutes to figure out how to manage all four kids *and* teach a class.

This called for the only thing I could think of. Bribery.

Which was how I ended up in the dollar store with four children in tow.

"Alright, Petries. Each of you can get ten items." I had two twenties in my wallet and figured that would give them enough things to last for one fifty-minute lecture. If they got bored with one toy, they could move on to the next one nine times. "Here's the thing. You need to pick all ten toys in less than a minute. Go!"

It was like watching hyenas strip a carcass.

I led my troop to the register. "Ollie, stop trying to trip everyone."

"I'm not!"

"You are. I watched you do it." She nearly succeeded with me.

"You're blind as a bat," came Ollie's sassy retort.

I was about to refute her claim but remembered Sarah's words to ignore her. It was the only way Ollie would let something go. Lo and behold, it worked.

The woman at the register scanned the items and put them into the reusable bag I'd supplied.

I checked the amount on the screen, my brow furrowing as the math failed to add up. "Um… I think you're doing it wrong."

The woman smacked her gum, not stopping to correct her mistakes.

"Excuse me," I said a little louder. "Everything is ringing up at one dollar and twenty-five cents."

"Inflation." Another pop of a bubble.

"But—" I quickly attempted to multiply forty items times a dollar and a quarter without a calculator and failed miserably. "I didn't plan on spending that much."

"What do you want to put back?" The woman waved to the items she'd already scanned.

"No, Mommy!" Ollie got between me and the counter.

"Nothing. It's fine. Everything's going to be fine." I scrounged for another twenty in the secret pocket where I kept my emergency money, my mind boggling how it was even possible to spend that much at a dollar store. Would a nanny cost fifty bucks an hour?

"I'm hungry," Fred whimpered as the cashier was handing me a ten in change.

"Shoot. Snacks. We'll need snacks."

I tucked the ten in the wallet and produced a credit card for the twenty bucks in snacks because I didn't have the heart to fight Olivia on all her choices. By the time we were done, we were running out of the store to get to campus. It was now ten minutes behind the time I thought we'd be done, not to mention thirty dollars over budget. That was the thing with kids. You always needed to add time—and money—to even the simplest of tasks.

However, we didn't have much time. We arrived at

campus with hardly a minute to spare and little more than a half-baked plan as to how to keep the kids busy while I taught. I nearly leaped for joy when I discovered the conference room next to where I had to lecture was empty, and according to the schedule, it wouldn't be in use until well after my class was done.

Empty room plus toys and snacks equaled a godsend.

"Listen up, Petries. I need all of you to stay in this room while Mommy teaches a class. Fred and Ollie, what does that mean?"

"We stay here," Fred said as if that was crystal clear.

Ollie simply scowled.

"You have enough toys and snacks to last fifty minutes. Fifty." In other words, the number of dollars it now cost to buy forty dollars' worth of dollar store shit. I displayed all five fingers on one hand and made a zero with my other to drive the number home. "You have to be good for all of those minutes. No funny business."

"Or what?" Ollie shot back.

"Or we won't go for ice cream afterward." Until that moment, I had not fully intended to take them for ice cream. Now I was committed, which meant at least another twenty-five dollars. Thirty if anyone got a waffle cone, and I sure as hell intended to with the way the day was going. Sprinkles, too. Which meant today's outing was threatening to come in at a hundred bucks. Sarah was making $136 to teach for the day, which meant once we subtracted the cost of toys, treats, and taxes, we were pretty much net zero.

Awesome.

At least the promise of ice cream got Ollie to sit on the floor with her coloring book. I was taking it as a win.

I edged out of the door, wondering if I could lock it but knowing that would be illegal. Possibly immoral, too, but definitely illegal. I wasn't entirely certain if leaving four unattended kids in the room next to where I would be without locking the door broke any laws, but I didn't have time to worry about it.

"Hello, everyone," I said to the class, shoving my legal questions out of my mind for the time being. "I'm Dr. Petrie, and I'll be filling in today."

There was some shuffling of feet but no arguments from the students. Another reason why I preferred other people's kids when they became adults. Adults rolled with the punches. You almost never had to bribe them with trips to the so-called dollar store.

I launched into my lecture, and thirty minutes in, I couldn't believe how everything was working out. At first, my kids had been a little loud, but they'd settled down, and I hadn't heard a peep for several minutes now. I only had twenty—no, nineteen minutes to go.

Dr. Arden walked in with a worried expression. She approached me and whispered into my ear, "We have a globe situation."

"A global situation?" My heart raced. How was this possible? I hadn't even gotten the opportunity to break ground on the bunker. I needed more time to prepare before the world ended.

"No, globe. As in your children have gotten ahold of the globe from Dr. Hicks' room and are rolling it down the stairwell. Then bringing it back up and rolling it down again."

"They escaped from the conference room?" I knew I should have locked it.

"What conference room?"

"Where are they now? I should go get them." I turned to my computer, with all my notes.

"Go. I'll take over here."

"Are you sure? I mean, if you have a plan for retrieving the—"

"No." Fear danced in Dr. Arden's eyes. "I already tried getting the globe on my own, but your eldest daughter is feisty."

"I'm so sorry," I babbled. "Sarah had to work today. My parents couldn't help. I didn't know what to do. It's not my normal day."

"I know, Lizzie. I'll be fine here. Just get your children."

She didn't have to say *under control*. I knew that was what she meant.

The closer I got to the stairwell, the louder the noise grew. How had I missed that?

"Olivia Rose Petrie!" I shouted when I saw her with

the globe in her hands, about to roll it down the stairs again. "Give me that globe right now, young lady!"

The three other kids wore terrified expressions, the younger ones stepping behind Freddie.

Not my Ollie Dollie, who had an evil streak. "No."

"Yes." I shook my outstretched hands.

"I want ice cream."

"Bad children don't get ice cream."

"I'll tell Mom you called me bad. She doesn't like talk like that." The kid was playing some serious three-dimensional chess.

"I'll tell Mom you got me in trouble with my boss," I countered. "How do you think I pay for your ice cream? By working. Now, give me that globe right this instant, or you'll never have ice cream ever again in your life!"

Check. Mate.

To my astonishment, she actually complied.

"Now, let's get your toys and scram." Before I got into even more trouble at work.

By the time I got all of them into the car, I collapsed over the steering wheel. "All you four had to do was stay in the room. Now everything's a mess. How am I going to explain this to your mother?"

"I won't tell her," Fred said. He was always on my side.

Demi seconded it.

Calvin nodded.

Ollie simply stated, with arms crossed and a determined stare, "Ice cream."

"If I get you ice cream, you pinky swear you won't tell mom?" I whispered.

"You won't tell on me?"

"I agree." Like I was going to tell. Sarah would probably rip my head off for leaving our children unattended, but what did she expect me to do in a pinch? "Do you?"

Through the rearview mirror, I watched Ollie nod in agreement.

Day one of splitting duties fifty-fifty and I already wanted to toss in the towel.

How did Sarah do this every single day?

CHAPTER EIGHT

"Why exactly do the twins have a playdate today?" I demanded of Sarah as I pulled a T-shirt over my head. "They went to yet another birthday party yesterday. Tonight, we're having a family barbecue. Why add a playdate on top of that? All I've been doing for two weeks is ferrying the kids from one thing to another."

"Because they're kids, and they need to stay active." Sarah angrily brushed her hair, sitting on the bench in our bathroom. "Welcome to my world."

"I didn't do this much shit all the time when I was a kid," I argued.

"And look how you turned out." The way Sarah said it, I had a feeling it wasn't intended to be a compliment. "By the way, your shirt's on backward."

I glanced down at my *That's what I do. I read history, and I know things* tee, which indeed was backward because I couldn't see the quote on the front but in the standing mirror behind me. "I'm surprised you told me. You clearly want to punish me for not adulting to your impossible standards."

"Yep. That's exactly my evil plan, which I will keep doing forever because goodness knows you never like learning anything that isn't in a frigging history book." Sarah stood and left the bathroom, a wave of hostility in her wake.

I shook a fist at her retreating back. I couldn't help wondering why she was so pissed at me. She was getting what she wanted, working outside the house and having her precious grown-up time. I was the one who was suffering. If anyone was going to be hostile, it should've been me.

Thirty minutes later, Freddie, Ollie, and I stood on the front steps of the address Sarah had punched into my GPS, fearful I'd go to the wrong address even though this was the exact same house where we'd attended the over-the-top castle birthday party a few weeks before. As much as I hated admitting this, Sarah wasn't far off the mark because getting lost was something I excelled at. Unfortunately for me, no one seemed to admire that as a skill.

Oh no. They loved to see the negative in everything.

The door swung open, and there stood a woman roughly my age, with makeup caked on her face like she'd used a spatula. It took a full three seconds for me to recognize her as Ingrid, the woman I had met before. She was wearing a Tory Burch striped crochet knit polo and Hudson jeans, and the only reason I knew that was because Sarah had become quite obsessed with those brands in this past year. In fact, Sarah had talked about them so much I'd actually thought Tory Burch was the name of one of the moms in the playgroup. It took me weeks to figure out why she got so huffy every time I asked about Tory, but when she finally caught on I wasn't trying to be a jerk and was just ignorant of the brand, I was forced to endure an eternity of looking through fashion photos online. I'd almost preferred when she'd believed me to be an insensitive cow.

Personally, I thought the stuff was hideous, even on Sarah, though I would never say that out loud because while I may be stupid sometimes, I'm not *that* stupid. Honestly, though, between the never-ending tunics and the clothes that made all the middle-aged women look like they'd raided their teenage daughter's closets, I wasn't sure what was worse. If I was going to dress too young for my age, you could bet I would be doing it in cartoon T-shirts.

"Lizzie, it's wonderful to see you," Ingrid greeted me, not meaning a word of it. She gave me a not so casual once-over, taking in my black flip-flops, shorts, and nerdy T-shirt. I suddenly remembered my outfit not fitting in the last time I was here. Was that what

Sarah meant about me only learning from history books and not shirts about history?

"Likewise. Reporting to playdate duty." I actually fucking saluted the snobby bitch. Even Freddie half-rolled his eyes, and I swear Ollie wanted to kick me in the shins for being so annoying.

Luckily, Ingrid laughed and responded with a salute.

Seriously, I wanted to puke my guts up. I hadn't been this nervous since defending my dissertation.

"Kiddos, you know the drill." Ingrid waved them inside.

This time Freddie saluted, and I wanted to hug my son, but before I could engage my brain, both twins were off like a shot into the backyard.

"Shouldn't I—" I pointed toward where the kids disappeared. I sorta remembered Sarah mentioning this playdate involved swimming. Sure, the twins had taken swim lessons, but I didn't like them in a pool without adult supervision. Had Ingrid heard of my lack of adulting abilities, or was it my outfit choice that had given me away?

"Don't worry. My nanny and au pair are with the kids. Come with me to hang with the moms." She said it like I wasn't actually one of the moms, but they'd make an exception this one time. "Is Sarah unwell?"

"No. She, uh, had other plans." I followed the *click-clack* sounds of the woman's strappy heels, wondering how she walked so perfectly in those death traps. They couldn't be comfortable.

Tittering assaulted my ears before we rounded the wall, and then the root cause of a lot of Sarah's hangups from the past several months slammed into me like a wrecking ball to the gut. Every single woman wore nearly identical knitted tops, jeans, and sandals with heels like it was some kind of mommy playdate uniform. This had to be a bad Barbie-movie dream, right? Surely grown women wouldn't want to look like they all belonged to a suburban mom cult.

"Would you like a mimosa?" Ingrid asked.

"Virgin," I said, unable to remember the names of all the moms in the room even though I'd been around them a few times at the recent birthday parties. It should be a rule that if you dressed the same and wore the same hairdo and makeup you must wear a name tag for us normies.

"Pardon?" Beneath her layers of foundation, Ingrid had gone a bit pale. "That's just orange juice."

"I guess it is." Why I hadn't realized it before I opened my mouth was a great question I wish I had the answer to. "I don't want alcohol."

"You don't drink?" This was whispered, but everyone in the room must have heard, given all conversation ground to a halt. Everyone turned to gawk at me, the weirdo in the room.

"Never. Er, before five, that is," I quickly added

after the gasps. You'd have thought I'd admitted to hunting puppies for sport.

"It's always five somewhere," one of the moms said, not adding a laugh because she was as serious as a heart attack.

"True, but I—" I shrugged, wanting to pull the rip cord on this adulting experience. What did Sarah see in these people?

It struck me at this moment that they all had exactly the same color hair. How was it possible? I wondered if they used the same stylist. I could picture them walking in one after the other and demanding, "Give me the Ingrid."

There was the squeal of kids. Happy squealing. Splashing. More squealing.

Fuck me. Sarah probably hated this as much as I did but did it all the time so our kids had access to a private pool with their friends.

No wonder my wife wanted to rip my head off these days. She might succeed in a roundabout way because if I had to spend time with these lionesses in heels on a regular basis, I might decapitate myself to end the misery.

That was my solution to everything I didn't like. Not actually removing body parts but cutting out aspects I didn't enjoy, leaving Sarah to handle all the things I hated.

As I pondered this shortcoming of mine, a fancy glass of orange juice was placed in my hand.

"Have you gotten your tickets to the Halloween charity event yet?" Another mom asked me, and I guessed it was because she was on the edge of the party as well. Was she new? On the outs with the sect? How could I casually explain to her that talking to me wasn't going to make her look good with these Kool-Aid swilling moms?

"Uh, probably. Sarah is the most organized person I know." And patient and loving. I had a lot of serious making up to do for the rest of my life if I survived this playdate. My lack of fifty-fifty parenting had put her through the wringer.

"Now that you mention it," the mom said, "I think she's on the committee."

I bobbed my head, pretending I knew that tidbit, but it didn't register at all. Sarah liked to call me adorably clueless, but I couldn't see the adorable part at the moment. Cruel was more like it. How many committees had my poor wife joined?

Halloween charity. I prayed it was something we'd take the kids to, where they had to wear costumes. Not the parents, or more specifically, not me. Yes, my favorite song was "Monster Mash," but that was where my Halloween spirit ended. A girl's got to have some pride. I did not do costumes. I had a feeling everyone in the room was into matching costumes and family-themed spectacles. They could count me out.

The woman, whose name I had neglected to ask, jumped ship, skirting over to two moms deep in a conversation. I edged closer to the wall, hoping to blend into the floor-to-ceiling painting that looked like a child had made it but had probably cost more than my teaching salary for the past decade.

The doorbell rang again, and the host—I think it was her, anyway, since I still couldn't tell anyone apart—departed. She quickly returned with the normal mom I'd met at the castle birthday party. This time, the host pointed to me. "There's Lizzie."

Tracy made her way over to me, accepting her mimosa without asking for no booze. Wise woman. I was starting to see why alcohol was a must at these gatherings. It would take the edge off, if nothing else.

"Hey," I said, noticing that while Tracy didn't wear a T-shirt and flip-flops—in other words, she'd put more effort into her outfit than I had—she fell far short of the required uniform. "I didn't get the dress code memo." I tugged on the hem of my shirt.

"Neither did I."

"At least your shirt has a collar."

"To hide my third nipple."

My eyebrows shot upward. "How does that work?"

She laughed. "Sorry. I'm nervous. I make stupid, nonsensical jokes when nervous."

"Me too. If we plan to survive today, we need to stick together."

We clinked our glasses to seal the pact.

Tracy moved closer to me. "I don't think that's

going to be a problem. It seems we've been deemed the pariahs."

I glanced around, not making eye contact with a single person, and not for lack of effort. "I've noticed that. How's your son?"

"He loves swimming, so hopefully he's having fun. Is Fred here?"

"Yep, and Olivia. She'll protect both of them if need be."

"Will she save us?" Tracy asked wryly.

"I haven't tested that theory, yet. She's good at tossing me under the bus to get her way, but I have a feeling if others ganged up on me, she'd deal with them. She takes after her mom—er, Sarah. Neither of them takes shit from others. Well, that's not entirely true. She lives with me, and clearly I'm a very slow learner." I glanced down at my outfit as if presenting exhibit one in the case against myself.

Tracy laughed. "Are you new to the neighborhood?"

"Not really. We moved here right before the pandemic. You?"

"We moved a few months ago. From Idaho. This place is wild." Tracy sipped her mimosa. "My husband got a teaching job at Harvard. Astrophysics. We thought living outside of Boston and Cambridge would be easier. Neither my husband nor son likes crowds."

"I'm not a fan either," I admitted as if she hadn't already guessed this about me. "It's been hard finding a place to fit in, though."

"I'm having a get-together in a couple of weeks if you'd like to come." She must have registered the fear in my eyes because she hastily added, "No one from this party will be there."

My brain whirred into action, trying to concoct a friendly way to decline, but then Sarah's voice in my head said, "Say yes. You need a friend, ya moron." Sarah probably wouldn't have added the last bit, but I felt like I deserved it. Slow learner, indeed.

"That'd be great." I raised my drink to my lips, wishing it was water because the acid in the orange juice was doing a number on my nervous stomach, which was twisting into more knots with each passing second.

At least I could go home and tell Sarah I had plans with a potential friend. Doing this without gloating or sticking my tongue out was going to be a challenge. Why did adulting have to be so fucking hard?

CHAPTER NINE

That night, I hid in the library, also known as my office, trying to focus on my script for an upcoming podcast episode. Truth be known, I was simply staring into space.

For days, I'd been running myself ragged, watching the kids, turning in end-of-the-semester grades, and helping out around the house. Now that I had time to focus on the one task that absolutely had to get done before bed, my brain was shrouded in a fog so deep I didn't think I'd ever have a rational thought again.

"Earth to Lizzie!" Sarah stood on the other side of my desk, waving her arms.

"Sorry." I shook my head slightly, but the fog remained. "Did you say something?"

She came around the desk and placed her hands on my shoulders, kneading them. "You look tired."

"You have no idea."

Sarah leaned down and kissed the back of my neck, but I brushed her away.

"What's wrong?"

"I'm sticky. I've been sticky for two solid weeks. Yesterday, I had to run to the store, and it wasn't until I was in line that I noticed I had a yogurt handprint on the back of my jeans, and I didn't give a flying fuck. Me. I used to cry when I had anything gross on me. Now, I'm wandering around in the world, gooey from head to toe."

"You aren't sticky here." She nipped at my earlobe.

I pulled away. "Please. Don't."

"Have it your way," Sarah muttered. She perched herself on the edge of my desk. "How was the playdate?"

"I'm pretty sure the twins had a blast. Both fell asleep in the car on the short drive back."

"How did your playdate go?" She nudged my knee with her bare foot.

"I don't have playdates." I bristled, wondering if Ingrid had texted Sarah asking her never to send me in her stead again?

"That well, then." Sarah leaned back on her arms, stretching her back in a blatant attempt to show me her goods.

I wasn't in the mood. Not at all.

"Why are moms so mean?" I rested the back of my head on the chair, training my eyes on the ceiling because Sarah was right about her boobs. They were my kryptonite, and any other time I would have been glad for the distraction. Tonight, however, the only thing I wanted to feel was annoyed.

"I'm a mom. Are you putting me in that category?"

"At the moment, yes. You knew I'd hate it."

"Truth."

I met her eyes. "Then why'd you make me go?"

"Why do I always have to be the one who goes?"

"You get along with them."

"Only because I have to for the kids' sake. You did get along with them, didn't you?" The accusation was etched into the lines around her mouth.

"I tried. I think they slipped booze into my virgin mimosa. It's not kind."

Sarah sat up straight, ready to take on a fighting stance. "You really think they did that?"

"I can't prove it, and if they did, it was only a small amount. But, yeah… I felt a little funny after." This was a stretch of the truth, and I knew it, but I also wished it was true. It would have made a great explanation for why I had been so bad at fitting in, other than the obvious. I was completely useless when it came to being human.

"You told them you don't drink," Sarah pressed, all the feistiness she'd been channeling into enticing me with her boobs suddenly redirected toward righting this wrong. Who was I to correct her?

"I said I didn't drink at that time of day. I shouldn't have to explain why I don't drink." I crossed my arms, firm in my conviction that there probably had been champagne in that orange juice, even if I hadn't been able to taste it and couldn't prove it was there. They just seemed the type to play a trick like that, and nothing would change my mind. "They're a bunch of mean girls. And what's up with them all dressing the same? It's creepy. We never had to deal with that in Colorado."

"Wellesley is a much different beast than Fort Collins."

"Are you happy here?"

"Yes. Aren't you?" Concern slammed into her eyes. Now that she'd claimed she was happy, I almost regretted bringing it up. But I couldn't lie.

"Sometimes I wonder if we made a mistake moving to such a pretentious place. I don't want my kids to grow up thinking getting sloppy drunk at a Sunday morning playdate is a normal thing to do. I'd thought the mean moms in Fort Collins were bad. These women—they're different. Like they can sniff out fear a hundred miles away. Sure, they smile and nod when I speak, but they do it in such a harmful way. I don't want our Petrie troop to turn out like that."

"I don't think moving back to Colorado is the solution. People are people. It's our job to raise our children so they don't turn into monsters."

Sarah said this as if it were that easy, but we couldn't get Ollie to behave now. What would she be like in twenty years?

"If you think the moms in the social group are monsters, why did you send me there?"

"To show you why I need a job," she said quietly, almost pleading. "I have to have normal adult interaction."

"You teach high school. Last time I checked, teenagers aren't normal or adults."

"Last time I checked, neither are you." She didn't wait for a response, standing as if to leave the room.

"That may be the case," I said, not wanting her to leave and hoping as long as I kept talking, she wouldn't. "But thank goodness you only have a couple weeks left to this teaching gig, and then life around here can go back to normal."

"Back to normal?" Sarah paused mid step, turning toward me. She was staying, but now I wondered if I'd miscalculated. Her tone was sharp enough to cut through glass. "What's normal for you? Because I get that whole not feeling attractive when you feel sticky all the time. That's *my* normal. I've been covered in yogurt and apple sauce for six years now. These past two weeks, teaching—I'm starting to feel like my old self again. And, you know what? I like it."

She did have a glow to her. I wondered if I had looked like that before all these new duties started weighing me down. Before the yogurt fingers and mean moms with their mimosas, had I glowed, too? Had Sarah stolen my glow? I doubted there was enough for the both of us.

"The kids need you," I said, shifting my argument to one that might be more likely to work. "I need you. I don't like the mean moms. The kids are impossible sometimes. This has been a nightmare. I would think you'd understand how hard it is for me. I want my wife back. None of these things seem to bother you."

"Do you even hear yourself right now?" Speaking of glowing, Sarah's eyes were on fire, but in that way cartoon demon eyes turned red before they started shooting lasers at people. "You act like this is all about you. Do you think I have a magical formula or something? I don't like the petty moms, either. They're constantly fighting, trying to one-up each other, and the worst part is I started to become one of them. You don't need to tell me how hard it is to raise four kids because I've been doing it a lot longer than two weeks. I've been a second-class citizen for years now. Not seen as Sarah, an individual, but as a mom. You only see me as a wife, but what you really mean is mom, too, because you want me to take care of you just like you're one of the kids. Do you know since we moved here, you haven't tried to fit in? You've made zero attempts to make friends—"

"I'm friends with Willow," I pleaded, hoping the only example I could come up with would be enough to make her stop her ranting before I got a laser beam to the face.

"She's Maddie's girlfriend. She moved into our house. That doesn't count. You've depended on me for everything, including your own entertainment and circle of friends. It's exhausting."

I scrunched my face. "I don't like your friends."

"I'm not talking about the mean moms. I'm making friends at the school, new friends, and I don't want to feel guilty about that. I want to see my friends and not worry that you're home alone feeling sorry for yourself, because you excel at that. The whole *woe is me* routine is draining!"

"For your information, I made a friend." I couldn't believe I hadn't thought of it before, but it's hard to concentrate when a glowing demon lady is yelling at you. "Tracy invited me to a get-together. I was going to ask if you could come along, but now I'm not. You clearly don't want to be around me. I'm baffled why you came in here thinking I'd put out when I'm exhausted."

"Because you've never done that to me." The needle on the sarcasm meter started to spin with that one, and Sarah probably had a point, only I was in no mood to think about it. "I don't know where you've been for the past six years, but it hasn't been here."

"You just said I never go anywhere or do anything. Now you say I haven't been here. Which is it?" I'd started my retort with an air of triumph, but by the time I'd closed my mouth, I already knew I was in hot water from the way Sarah closed her eyes and sucked in oxygen like it was the only thing keeping her from a nuclear meltdown.

"I don't care where you were physically. You clearly haven't been present in my life emotionally. I'm tired of coddling you." She opened her eyes, and I kinda wished she hadn't. The sudden calm was more terrifying than the anger. "There's a rumor at the school that the teacher I'm subbing for won't be back next school year. If they offer me the job, I'm taking it. It'll be my own class. My lesson plans. My chance to revive my career. Because you might be excited for my gig, as you call it, to end, but I'm dreading summer. I need to be Sarah again. Not mom. Not wife. But Sarah."

"Why can't you be all three?"

"Because you're doing such a fantastic job of managing that right now? You think taking the kids for a walk once in a while, teaching them about women in history, makes you mom of the year. I have news for you, Lizzie. You have no idea how hard it is to be a full-time mom. But mark my words. I will make you understand if it's the last thing I ever do!"

With that, she stormed out of the office, leaving me to absorb everything she'd said. With my brain fog, I didn't think much would make sense for a very long time. Maybe it'd sink in when she served me with divorce papers.

CHAPTER TEN

Willow bounded into the room with extra pep in her step. This was a feat. She was the type of extra-exuberant person who in all probability in a former life was a rainbow-farting unicorn. I couldn't imagine how much self-affirmation or whatever it would take for her to reach this energy level. "Are you ready to podcast? I'm ready to podcast." She bounced on her feet, like a boxer ready for the big match. "We're going to kill it!"

I answered with a frustrated grunt, staring at the thirty-eight reminders on my phone that hadn't been taken care of, ranging from *scoop cat litter* to *order groceries*, something I had previously failed at miserably by accidentally duplicating, or triplicating, my order and not realizing until all the deliveries arrived on my doorstep. I was sure Sarah assigned me this task because she knew I would fail even though she said she trusted I wouldn't do it again. That was a surefire way I would screw it up, by telling me I wouldn't.

Nevertheless, the task had been assigned to me, along with all the others. When was I going to get everything done? Whatever magic Willow had found to boost her energy, I would happily have paid her to share the secret, as long as it wasn't some type of weird hippy-dippy mantras because come on; those didn't work. Or did they? Did self-belief type exercises work? Sure, I was the type to boast about shit, but deep within the bowels of my self-esteem, the only emotion that propelled me from one task to the next was a dreadful sense of failure. I thought I was a failure, despite my accomplishments, and it was only a matter of time for all the bad to come to light. How long until everyone in my life forced me to walk through the crowds so people could taunt me by calling me a fraud?

Fraud. Fraud. Fraud.

Willow again tried to prod me out of my funk by saying, "Isn't it wonderful we get to podcast together? I love this time."

Who had time? Didn't the rainbow-farting unicorn know I was losing precious seconds? As if fate wanted to confirm this, another reminder dinged on my phone. It was car inspection time. Great. It'd take at least an hour to have a mechanic kick the tires and test the headlights.

"We need to turn that frown upside down." Willow

twisted her fingers into her cheeks like that was all it took to make me smile.

I glared at her. If she dared come closer with those fingers of hers, I was prepared to bite.

Willow took her seat but didn't put her headphones on when I did. Instead, she stared at me, and when I didn't say or do anything, she mimed for me to take my headphones off.

Begrudgingly, I did, despite sweat forming on my back. I was so stressed about all those damn reminders I could barely function.

"What's wrong?"

"Sarah and I fought last night, and she was pretty mean, telling me I don't have friends and that it's exhausting being around me." My lips curled into a snarl. "All of this isn't easy for me. Everything is easy for her. I have to work extra hard, but she can't see that."

Willow tilted her head slightly. "Why do you think everything's easy for her?"

"Because she does everything with such ease. You can drop her into any social situation, and she'd be able to talk about any subject without making things weird. Me—I take awkward to an extreme, making everyone uncomfortable, including myself."

"I don't think that's true, but let's put a pin in that for now. How did the fight start?"

"She wants to work full-time again."

Willow waited.

I motioned that was it.

The corners of Willow's lips turned downward. "You two fought about Sarah working again? Why? She loves being back in the classroom. Haven't you noticed how light and bubbly she's been?"

"She might be"—I smacked my hand against my chest—"but I'm not. I'm exhausted all the time. It's hard babysitting four kids."

Willow acted out *back the fuck up* along with the beeping sounds. "Babysit? They're your kids. You don't babysit your own children."

It was only hearing my words coming back at me from Willow's mouth that it occurred to me if anyone else had said what I said about their own children, I would have been very mad indeed. "I didn't mean it that way. My brain doesn't seem to want to fully engage. I'm in a perpetual fog. If Sarah goes back to work full-time, how will I manage? The first day she went back, I thought for sure I was going to get fired."

"What happened?"

I explained how I had to take the kids to campus and the globe incident that had resulted. "I used to love globes, but now, whenever I see the one in the library, I start shaking with fear. I'm not a good mom. Only a few weeks of filling Sarah's shoes and I'm starting to resent my children. And my wife. I don't know how I'll manage, and it's scaring me."

Willow bobbed her head, staring past me. A habit of hers when deep in thought.

The silence was killing me, so I tried to fill it. "We have a strong support system, but if Sarah goes back to teaching permanently, it's not fair to expect everyone else to pitch in so much."

"You can always hire someone to help."

"An actual babysitter?" My front tooth sank into my lower lip.

"What about a nanny?"

"No." I shook my head. "No. It should be one of us. And… and Sarah is better at it."

"Did you say that to her? Please tell me you didn't."

I laced my fingers, fidgeting. "Not in those words, but maybe I—"

Willow stopped me with a raised hand. "Don't tell her that. I need you to hear me. For weeks, you've been doing what Sarah has been doing for six years—"

"The twins aren't six yet."

"They will be in August, and that's not the point. You want Sarah to give up a job she loves so you aren't inconvenienced. Do you not see how insensitive that is? Why should you have your career, but not Sarah? And don't give me the bullshit line that Sarah's better at it. She's just had more time doing it."

"What about her friend comment?" I chewed on my bottom lip, which was dry, but I hadn't had time to search for my Chapstick.

"I agree with her. You need friends. She needs friends. Some can be mutual friends, but it's healthy for both of you to have separate people you can rely on. Not only will it give you time away from each other, but it'll give you two more things to talk about when you're together. You can't simply be around your family all of the time. Friends make one's life richer."

I let out a breath, my shoulders slumping. "Do you really think Sarah's been happier lately?"

"One hundred percent."

My nose wrinkled at this unwanted response. "Because of teaching?"

"Part of it. Look, I'm not a parent. I'd like to be one day, but I know it's a hard job. Most moms I know feel invisible and bitter."

"She called herself a second-class citizen," I admitted in a hushed tone. I'd almost forgotten that part, which made it all the worse. How could the woman I loved feel like that, finally tell me, and then I didn't even remember?

"That's got to be a terrible feeling," Willow said. All I could do was nod. "I'm afraid Sarah's very good at hiding her own struggles. You haven't seen the half of it, but it's still enough that you know you don't want to do it."

"What does that mean?" My heart pounded as I considered the possibility Sarah was hiding things from me.

"Everything you find hard, I guarantee you, Sarah finds it just as hard."

"Impossible." I shook my head, unable to consider the notion. "She doesn't look it."

"She's not Mary Poppins, Lizzie." Willow didn't usually sound exasperated, but she did now, and I was the cause. "No one is perfect. Things are hard for everyone, even if they don't show it."

I sat quietly for a long moment, letting this concept digest before saying a word. "If I'm understanding what you're saying, I need to accept the fact Sarah wants to go back to work, and I also need to do a better job to make friends that aren't in my family or living under my roof?"

"Those would be good steps forward."

"Good steps? That means not all the steps." Proud of myself for coming up with that bit of insight all on my own, I picked up my pen, ready to take notes. "I would like to know *all* the steps, so have at it."

Willow made a snorting sound. "You crack me up, you know that."

I shook my pen as way of saying I wasn't joking. Who had time for that?

"When's the last time you and Sarah had alone time?"

I swallowed, wondering what she meant by that. Alone, like an empty house? Or was she talking about sex? My cheeks began to tingle as I recalled how I'd rebuffed Sarah's advances. I couldn't admit that to Willow.

"We went away to the Berkshires recently," I said instead.

A look of horror crossed Willow's face. "That was years ago!"

"Was it?" I tensed with panic, like a kid who'd given the wrong answer on a pop quiz. "I guess you're right. It's hard to get away, especially during the school year. Over winter break, it's the holidays, and that's a miserable time because we're trying to do everything to make the kids have a wonderful holiday. Of course, neither of us gets to enjoy it. It's more an endurance thing. It seems that's what marriage and family life is. An endurance test that never ends. I meet one deadline and then gird for the next. I'm exhausted."

"I don't know how to say this"—Willow put a hand on my arm and gave it a squeeze— "but it's only like that if you're doing it wrong."

CHAPTER ELEVEN

It was the night of Tracy's party, and the thought of attending all on my lonesome was freaking me out. Sure, I knew Tracy a little by now, but I didn't know any of the other people who were going to be there. This was the perfect recipe for disaster for the likes of me—the clueless one.

"Last chance to have a romantic night with me." I attempted to waggle my brows at Sarah, but I think the end result only made me look like I was having a seizure or something.

"How is going to a party romantic?"

"I was thinking I could skip the party—"

"Oh no, you don't." She offered me a *buck up* smile, adding, "It's good for you to try new things. I'm proud of you."

"How is a party new? I've been to parties before. Three birthday parties in the past month." I started to count them on my fingers. "Oh, don't forget the playdate."

"Those have been for the kids. I meant I'm proud of you for finally making friends here. You need friends. Go. Just be yourself, and everything will be okay."

"When has being myself ever worked out for me, or anyone unlucky enough to be in the room, for that matter?" I whined. "You don't even like me right now, and you're required by law to do so."

"That's not exactly how marriage works, FYI. Also, I always like you, even when you're whining. Now, go." Sarah made a shooing motion with her hands. "I'm looking forward to a night to myself. The kids are at mom's until tomorrow afternoon. I want to take a long bubble bath. Read a book. Relax."

"That sounds nice." I blew out a frustrated raspberry.

"Lizzie, stop worrying so much. It's just a night out. Tracy seems absolutely lovely. If you end up hating it, at least you get credit for trying."

"I do?" I perked up. "I like getting credit."

"I thought that'd get your attention. You're going to be late."

I checked my watch. "Shit. Gotta run."

It wasn't far to Tracy's place, but the traffic was brutal. That was something I'd noticed on our drives in Massachusetts. Coming from Colorado, where most intersections were pretty straight forward, Massachusetts was terrifying. Think three lanes on one side, narrowing to one lane the minute you reached the other side. Everything in this state, from preschool applications to roads, seemed to be set up for dog-eat-dog competitions. I wasn't suited for that amount of pressure in every aspect of my life. Even Sunday drives were cutthroat. I hoped parties would not live up to this tradition.

I was somewhat put at ease when I pulled up to the address where my GPS told me to stop. Tracy lived in a modest Cape-style house that had probably been built in the 1950s. It was the type of property more and more people had been buying sight unseen to tear it all down and build something bigger. There was no sign of major renovations at her place, though, which meant the interior was probably cramped but had still cost a million dollars. That was as close as you could get to normal around here.

"Lizzie! I'm so glad you made it." Tracy offered a warm smile as she met me at the door. "Come in, and let me introduce you."

"This is a nice house you have," I said, not really looking around much. A house was a house. But I knew small talk was important, so I was trying my best. "Where's your son?"

"This isn't my house," Tracy said. "It's my friend Jen's. I'm helping her with the party tonight."

"Oh." Truly, I had nothing more to say, being thoroughly confused. But as I followed Tracy into the living room, I was relieved when I saw every other guest was smiling. And they weren't dressed in the Wellesley mean mom uniform, either. Two of them even wore T-shirts! The muscles in my shoulders unleashed a smidge. Maybe this was my crowd after all.

"No Sarah tonight?" asked one of the women.

"Was I supposed to bring her? No one told me that. She's having a Sarah night." I slanted my head like a confused puppy.

"No. I was just curious. She and I are on the Halloween ball committee." The woman shrugged *no biggie*.

"Right. I must remember to ask Sarah about that. Will I have to dress up?" Could someone stab me in the eye instead so I could get a doctor's note? Knowing Sarah, she'd throw on an eye patch and make me go as a pirate.

"Of course!" The woman said it like that was a good thing, immediately making me reassess the likelihood that these were my people. "There's going to be a competition. I believe Sarah has her heart set on the best couple costume."

"I could kill her." Did I say that aloud? "I mean, wouldn't that be a good costume. Me being an ax murderer, and I'm carrying Sarah's head around. Wait. How would that work? Clearly, I need to workshop that." And, stop babbling about wanting to behead my wife around people who didn't know about my peculiar ways. Someone was likely to call the cops, which might not be all bad. I wouldn't need to have friends in prison, and I'd get all my meals provided. It could be worse.

"Who among us hasn't wanted to whack their partner?" Tracy joked, and much to my surprise, everyone laughed, even me.

It felt fucking good.

Oh my God. Was this why people had friends?

"Help yourself to the drinks and snacks before we get started." Tracy motioned to the table set up in the dining room.

Started on what? Did I have to play charades or something? I absolutely hated party games, and I was kicking myself for not foreseeing this wrinkle. The home didn't have air conditioning and sweat started to pool under my tits. Frankly, I hadn't thought that was possible given their smallness, but that was before experiencing a New England summer without AC.

That was another thing about Massachusetts. The humidity made life miserable, yet no one would admit it. People pretended it was always cold here, even when it was in the 90s with humidity to match. Not owning an air-conditioner was the Yankee summertime equivalent of not turning on the heat in the winter. No wonder the drivers were so aggressive. No one got a decent night of sleep with windows open and the air like soup. From experience, the less sleep I got, the crankier I became. I would never understand this place.

"Everyone ready for the big event?" Tracy asked.

All of them nodded, so I did the same, noticing I seemed to be the only one who had no idea what the big event entailed. I was praying for grilled hot dogs or something.

"Jen, take us to your kitchen."

I hadn't expected that, and I prayed this wasn't a cooking party because I'd have to confess I nearly burned down our Colorado home baking a cake. The type from a box. Not that I tried cooking it in the box because that would have been idiotic. What I had done wasn't much better, though. It had to do with too much oil and time in the oven. I think. Honestly, it still baffled me.

"Don't judge me." Jen did a little ta-da movement, and my eyes bulged by the sight before me.

Her kitchen was dirty. So filthy I'm surprised the health department hadn't closed her down. Yes, I know they only inspected restaurants, but if they got word of this hazmat level type of destruction, they should absolutely intervene to protect everyone in the neighborhood.

"No worries at all. That's what tonight's about." Tracy put on long, yellow gloves.

Were we going to clean Jen's kitchen? Was this a weird version of Habitat for Humanity? I didn't do germs, dirt, or whatever toxic pollution was caked around the sink.

"By the end of this, your kitchen is going to

sparkle." Tracy winked. Was she a pixie with astounding powers? Or maybe just delusional?

I nervously looked around, relieved none of the others were putting on cleaning gloves. Two of them went back to the dining room for another round of cheese and crackers. How could they eat in such filth? I'd lost my appetite completely.

As the crowd of women looked on, Tracy filled a bucket with warm water. She took a tiny cap from a large bottle, measured out a miniscule amount of the contents, and poured it in. "This powerful cleaning product is environmentally friendly, and you only need a small amount for a job this size."

Yeah, right. She'd added about a drop. No way would that make a dent in this disaster area.

It was like I'd been sucked into an infomercial, and I didn't quite understand how I'd ended up in this position. Yet I couldn't look away. I wanted to see how this story would end. I suspected in tears, with a lot of grime mixed in. Either way, it was riveting.

The women oohed and aahed when Tracy tackled the oven. One swipe with the sponge revealed the original color, which could be best described as off-white. Perhaps in the beginning, it had been white, but actually, it looked like that almond color that used to be so popular. It would've looked almost new if it weren't so dated.

"There's a stove top under there," Jen joked about her own messy situation.

I had to admit it was pretty impressive, although I was still baffled as to why we were all gathered around the stove watching Tracy clean it like it was an Olympic sport.

Was Tracy pitching her cleaning services to her friends?

By the time she finished with the fridge, I was ready to whip out my checkbook and hire Tracy on the spot. While my house wasn't this messy, I'd been wanting to hire a new cleaning service for ages, but Sarah kept thwarting me by tying this to her request for a nanny, so we hadn't gotten very far.

I had to admit it was nice to be included in this bunch, unlike the mean moms from the playdate. When it came to social situations, I didn't know a lot, but if any of those moms knocked on my bunker door needing a safe place, I wouldn't let them in. Would it be possible to have Lou install a peep hole to watch the zombies tear the mean bitches apart? I made a mental note to ask her before construction began.

When everything was sparkling clean, Tracy ripped off her gloves and tossed a sponge into the blackish water in the bucket. "Now, that's what I call clean."

One of the guests said, eyeing the water, "When's the next biohazard collection day?"

Jen rested her head on Tracy's shoulder. "It's so embarrassing."

"Don't be embarrassed. You have a husband and

two boys who do nothing around the house to help you."

Geez, we had four kids, and our kitchen wasn't this bad. Would Sarah toss me into the useless column like Jen's husband?

"So, ladies, who wants to buy a bottle?" Tracy had a glean in her eye.

Did she mean I'd get to take the bottle home to clean myself? Not take Tracy home? I was frankly a little sad Tracy's cleaning skills weren't included in this deal. I'd been convinced the product was indeed magical because my skin no longer crawled. I'd still shower as soon as I got home just from being in the kitchen before it sparkled. Maybe I'd need three showers to feel somewhat normal again.

"It's environmentally friendly?" I asked. "That's not a gimmick?"

"One hundred percent." Tracy nodded to punctuate the honesty.

"I'll take three," I said.

There was laughter and smiles all around.

"I knew there was a reason I liked you." Tracy grinned.

As other women placed their orders, several of those in the group asked me for my phone number. I didn't know what to say. I'd never been popular in my life, but here I was, making friends left and right. I freely offered up my digits, feeling good about myself.

Sarah wanted me to make friends, and now I had a

whole group of women who wanted me. Not in an inappropriate way, although part of me wouldn't have minded if Sarah got a little jealous. This group of women all seemed so kindhearted.

I still hadn't wrapped my head around why Tracy had invited me to a party at Jen's house so I could observe her clean it from top to bottom, but it was far from the worst night I'd ever had. It was almost fun, really. Women in Massachusetts had odd ideas about what constituted fun and friendship. I'd gone to Ethan's house many times, and not once did I stand around to observe someone clean his kitchen.

But, as they say, when in Rome…

CHAPTER TWELVE

I RETURNED HOME FROM THE PARTY MUCH later than anticipated. Of course, that was partly because I hadn't realized how different get-togethers were here compared to back in Colorado. I hadn't factored in the hour-long cleaning demonstration, or the time it would take for everyone to place orders for the products. Afterward, though, the evening had settled into a more recognizable format as we crowded into Jen's front room, chatting, nibbling on snacks, and laughing. There was a lot of laughter.

"How was your night?" Sarah was sitting in her reading chair, and the light behind her was on, but from the redness in her eyes, she'd been sound asleep until the moment I walked through the door.

"It was good." I paused in surprise, realizing this was not a lie. I'd actually had a nice time, kitchen cleaning and all. "Weird but good."

Sarah's eyebrows went up. "Why weird?"

I weighed whether I should go into detail, but decided against it. Sarah was experienced in this type of thing, way more so than I was. She'd probably think I was an idiot for not knowing what went on at a typical girls' night in, which was what several of the women had called it. I'd barely known the term, showing what an absolute newbie I was. I didn't need my wife knowing any of that.

"There were pigs in a blanket," I said instead, scratching behind our cat's ear until Hank marched off annoyed. I could never win with that cat, or anyone really. "I've never seen those at a party food before."

"Oh." Sarah's forehead crinkled. "I guess that is a little weird. Maybe."

"Right? I was expecting chips and dip, not gourmet cuisine." I kissed my fingertips with flourish. "Delicious."

"Sometimes you're really adorable, you know?"

"You haven't seemed to think that about me lately." I couldn't hold back a pout.

Sarah rubbed her eyes. "I could say the same about you."

"True." I nodded thoughtfully, stroking my chin. "Of course, I've always been my toughest critic."

Sarah tossed a throw pillow at me. "That wasn't what I meant, and you know it."

"I *knew* that was why they called these throw pillows." I chuckled as I retrieved the projectile from the floor. As my laughter faded, my mood grew more serious. "It's been a difficult adjustment for me lately. Not just stepping up more but everything. Life seems so much harder. Darker. I'm constantly worried about our children's future. Will there be a planet?"

"Oh, the little things," Sarah joked.

"Exactly." I actually smiled at this instead of faking it, which felt good. It was the first time in a while that the burdens I'd been carrying didn't feel ready to crush me at any moment.

"You do love to torture yourself with everything." Sarah put a hand to her mouth but couldn't quite conceal a yawn. "I have drinks with friends from work on Wednesday night. I'll need your help. Is that okay?"

"Wednesday?" I pulled my phone from my pocket, my eyes widening at four unread text notifications. Each was from a different woman I'd met at the party, and all of them appeared to be invitations to other gatherings, though none for Wednesday. Putting the messages aside until morning, I opened my calendar. "Looks like I have a late afternoon meeting, but leave the kids arrangements with me. I'll ask my dad and Helen if they can watch the rug rats. Or Allen now that he's on summer break."

"Mom and Troy already are watching the little ones. Maddie is taking Ollie to dance, and Willow is taking Freddie to his music class."

"Oh. What do you need me for?" I should have

remembered Ollie's and Fred's lessons. No matter how many alarms I set on my phone, I could never keep up.

"Dinner. Everyone will get home around six. Can you handle heating up a frozen lasagna without destroying the kitchen this time?"

"Hey!" I shook a finger at her. "It was a cake that wrecked the kitchen. Not a frozen meal."

"You're not really helping your cause." Sarah stretched her arms over her head. "Have you heard back from Lou?"

"I'm happy to inform you I have a follow-up meeting tomorrow to go over the plans." A feeling of giddiness overtook me as I remembered that Lou would be showing me some final ideas for my bunker. I could hardly wait.

Sarah gave me a skeptical look. "Should Mom or your parents be there?"

"Uh…?" Most definitely not. The last thing I needed was anyone else finding out about my secret bunker and then ratting me out to my wife. "I think I can handle it."

"But my mom would be a good resource," Sarah argued. "Goodness knows how many times she's redone her houses over the years. And Helen has experience from her shops."

"We don't need any walk-in flower fridges," I cracked, laughing a little too exuberantly to cover my panic. If I didn't get her to drop this right now, the jig would be up.

"Good point." Sarah rolled her head, cracking her neck. She must have been really tired if she didn't catch on I was trying too hard to be funny. That was one of my tells when I was trying to get away with something, and we both knew it.

Was it possible she'd forget I'd mentioned the appointment with Lou at all? I couldn't see how I would sneak the inclusion of a full-sized bunker past any of our parental units. They'd be sure to ask questions and then tattle on me. Unless I asked Lou to prepare separate quotes. Surely, that would work. Technically, Sarah wanted the numbers for the basement, not the bunker. Yes, that was because she had absolutely no idea the bunker was a thing. I mean, I knew she could define the word, but she didn't know I was considering building one under our house.

I wanted to keep it that way.

"Oh, since you're in charge of cooking Wednesday, we need cleaning products for the kitchen." This statement had nothing to do with the basement. It was possible I was in the clear.

I lit up at the memory of three large bottles of concentrated cleaner in the back of my SUV. "Don't worry. I've already taken care of that."

Like, for the next several years. Did the stuff expire? Shoot. I should have asked that question.

"Color me impressed." Sarah yawned again.

I was almost certain this interrogation was coming to an end.

"That's a victory right there!" Okay, one last effort to erase the meeting with Lou from her mind, and I was in the clear. "Say, I was thinking. Maybe it's time we get serious about hiring someone to clean the house. We used to have Miranda. Now that the COVID risk is receding, it might be a good idea to help us cope with everything."

"So a housekeeper is hunky-dory in your world, but not a nanny?"

I stiffened, realizing I may have overplayed my hand. The last thing I wanted was to tiptoe around yet another argument this late at night. "Can you give me a chance? I know it hasn't been all that smooth with me stepping up, but I know I can do a better job with a little more time and patience. Everyone else is pitching in. I'm learning I need to do more."

"I appreciate that, Lizzie. I really do. But it's only going to get more complicated as the school year revs up again this September. You'll have exams and papers to grade. Willow will be back in the classroom. You both have the podcast. Then there are your TV appearances on JJ's show. I'm always ferrying the kids around. School. Music and dance lessons. Ollie's adding tennis, and somehow your dad has got Calvin interested in golf. The kids' calendar this fall is scary busy."

"Tell me about it." I let out my breath in a huff, slightly lightheaded at the thought of how much all that was going to cost. "By the time I get my first cup of tea down me, I have eighteen reminders on my phone, but this is the joy of being moms. I know you. Deep down, you love all this."

"That doesn't mean I wouldn't love it even more if we had a—"

"No nannies."

"I was going to say an au pair."

My expression settled into a frown. "That's just a fancy French way to say nanny."

"No, it's different," Sarah argued. "I was talking to Ingrid the other day about her au pair—"

"By all means," I grumbled. "If Ingrid has one, it must be all the rage. Will the au pair have to dress in Tory Burch tunics?"

Sarah glared at me. Deep down, I knew I deserved it. "The service she's using has been placing young people from all over the world with American families for over fifty years. Host families provide room and board, plus a stipend, in exchange for help around the house. It's a cultural exchange, which is very different than a traditional nanny situation. We wouldn't just be getting help with the kids. We would be teaching a young woman about American life. About democracy."

"Democracy?" I shot her a suspicious look. She was laying it on a bit thick. "I like democracy as much as the next person, but I don't know about inviting a stranger into our house. Besides, I think I read recently about an au pair in Boston who killed a baby. It doesn't sound safe to me at all."

"When did that happen?" Sarah asked in alarm.

"1996," I muttered, knowing the fact I had to go back three decades for an example was not going to help my case. I decided to try a different approach. "We don't get a lot of time as parents. When the kids grow up and leave, we'll miss these days."

"If they leave," Sarah replied, chilling me to my bones. What was that supposed to mean? She was quick to explain. "Children aren't leaving the nest these days, you know. Not many can afford housing on their own. I wonder if we should discuss with Lou about adding an apartment over the garage."

"Like an in-law apartment?" A flicker of a light bulb went off over my head. The idea wasn't clear quite yet, but there was something to what Sarah had said. My brain needed the necessary time to marinate and tease something out of it.

"Yes, but for the children." There was a warning in Sarah's tone, as if she knew before I did that I would try to take this idea and turn it to my advantage.

"You want our children to live above the garage? I don't even know if that's legal." My voice dropped to a whisper, and I scouted over my shoulder at the listening device on the far side of the room.

"Not now. I'm thinking of the future. It's been on my mind a lot lately. Keeping me up, really. How are we going to manage everything?"

"Leave the worrying to me. I'm a world class worrier. I think the apartment over the garage is a great idea. I can move my office there for now. That'll free up the library as a kid hangout spot."

"You'd give up your library?" Sarah seemed beyond shocked, given her wide eyes and fish mouth.

"They need more space to have friends over, alone time, and their toy collection grows each Christmas and birthday. In the interest of less squabbling and you staring daggers at me, yes. I can take Gandhi with me when I'm working there. He's getting pretty frail. Most mornings, I have to carry the little guy home."

"That's because you take him and the kids on a forced march."

"Exercise is good for the mind, body, and spirit. Speaking of, you know what else is good?" I'd hoped a flourish of my eyebrows would fill in the blank, but Sarah only reacted with a yawn, so I quickly added, "A good night's rest."

"Exactly my thought."

Clearly my eyebrow trick had lost its charm. I needed to up my seduction game if we were ever going to have sex again.

Sarah rose from her chair, reaching for the light switch. "I'll make sure my mom knows about the garage addition when she joins you for that meeting with Lou."

Fuck.

Despite my best efforts, she'd remembered after all.

CHAPTER THIRTEEN

My eyes felt like glue after staying up late trying to get ahead with my *work* work, which is to say *not* the kids or house stuff, that occupied most of all my time these days. It seemed bad manners to vacuum the house at midnight—my usual go-to when stressed—so I brainstormed ways to outsmart students who tried to do assignments using ChatGPT. That was the topic of our all-hands-on-deck Wednesday departmental meeting, and I wanted to go into it prepared.

After considerable thought, my big suggestion was going to be for us all to go back to handwritten essays. Yes, it seemed almost prehistoric in the twenty-first century, and I had sincere doubts that some of my students knew how to write with paper and pen, but it would work. Of course, then I would have to grade papers that were illegible as well as illiterate (the latter being a given).

Maybe they could use university computers that didn't have ChatGPT installed. That could do the trick, although I couldn't figure out a way to deal with the students who could get around that with a few taps of the keyboard. Where there was a will to cheat, there was a way. Some students spent more hours trying to find the *easy* solution than it would have taken them to do the work the right way.

As I poured hot water into my first cup of tea, which would not be the last for the day, an Ollie scream pierced my eardrum.

I stormed in the direction of the ruckus, finding all four kids in my office, aka the library, aka their favorite room in the whole damned house. "What's going on in here?"

"She hit me." Fred rubbed a red spot on his arm.

"You stole my LEGO." Ollie's fists were clenched.

Demi and Calvin watched from the sidelines, staying out of clobbering range.

Smart kids.

"Why are you in here?" I demanded. "You're supposed to be getting ready for school. It's the last day!"

Now I was getting worked up, making a bigger fuss than they had. It was enough to call in the big guns. Sarah's footsteps echoed as she ran toward the commotion.

"What's going on in here?" Sarah fastened the last button on her blouse as she stood in the doorway. "Why aren't you getting ready for school?"

"That was my question!" I couldn't explain why her asking the same thing irritated me, but it did. Everything right now was bugging the shit out of me. "All of you upstairs. Get dressed! Or I swear, heads will roll!" I sliced one hand into my other palm, guillotine style.

They all scattered, even Olivia, without a single peep of protest.

"Heads will roll?" Sarah rolled her eyes as she tucked in her blouse. "I particularly liked the guillotine part. Can't say I've ever done that with our children."

"You look nice."

"Good recovery."

I sighed, my whole body so tense I felt like I'd been tied into a knot. "How do you stop yourself from losing your cool with the kids?"

"Oh, I don't. Not always. You just don't see me do it. They will test your patience every chance they get." She turned around, holding her hands at the base of her neck. "Can you help me with my necklace?"

On the third attempt, I got it hooked. "Why so fancy today?"

"I have that interview."

"What interview?" I asked slowly, dread oozing through my veins.

"For the job next school year. I could have sworn I told you."

There was no way she had told me. I would've remembered. By the pink tint on her cheeks, she knew she was lying, too.

"The teacher isn't coming back, then?" I asked, making the strategic choice not to call her out on her bullshit. Not now, anyway. I'd been mentally preparing for this, and I hoped I didn't show any hint of nerves. We moved into the entryway, where the kids' backpacks were. I rifled through them to see if there were parental slips of any type.

"No. She's taking the full year off for extended maternity leave."

A sharp pain stabbed me in the chest, but I tried not to flinch. "You look amazing."

"What about confident? Knowledgeable?"

I swallowed. "Absolutely. You'll be the best teacher in the school. No. In all of Massachusetts."

"Thank you." She kissed my cheek, relief evident as her features relaxed. "Fred! Ollie! We have to go, or we'll be late."

"What's this?" I studied the printouts in my hands about surviving an emergency and how to prepare a survival kit.

"I think it's part of their summer project. I remember seeing an email about it."

"What happened to summer reading?" I scowled at the papers. "They're young. Why do we need to scare the crap out of them?"

"Because it's a scary world."

I didn't like it, but taking out my fear on Sarah wasn't going to help matters, not to mention it'd probably contribute to another argument. I couldn't muster the energy for that.

Instead, I said, "I packed you a lunch, along with a breakfast bar and piping hot coffee in your travel mug. It's all on the counter. Love you. Good luck with the interview."

I rushed up the stairs to make sure Calvin and Demi would be ready for daycare, a new thing we were trying out since we hadn't been able to put them in preschool at the beginning of the year because they hadn't had their vaccines yet.

By the time I arrived at the coffee shop close to the campus, Lou was already there.

"Sorry I'm late." I took a seat at the table.

"You aren't," she assured me. "I'm always early."

"Me too, which is why I normally beat people to any appointment. I'm going to get a chai." I got to my feet. "Do you want anything?"

"All set." She motioned to her half-full cup. "I only have one a day."

I shook my head slowly, unable to recall when one cup had been enough to power me through a full day. "You don't have kids, do you?"

"Nope." She laughed, the carefree laugh of a person who had only ever suffered a poor night's sleep of her own free will. I barely remembered what that was like.

After getting my hot cup of life-giving elixir and retaking my seat, I said, "Hit me with it."

"Here are some ideas I found." She scooted closer so I could see her tablet.

I scanned the photos of real-life bunkers, pointing to one in particular that caught my eye. "What's going on with this one? It's hard to make out."

"I like that one, too, because it's like a panic room," Lou said with obvious enthusiasm. "This is the door leading down to the bunker, but no one will be able to see it."

I leaned closer to the tablet. "Are you saying it'll be invisible?"

"To those who don't know what they're looking at."

My lips curled upward almost without my knowledge. "I can go into it, and no one would know where I am."

"That's the idea, right?"

I replayed the carnage in my office this morning and then imagined myself in a space no one in the house knew about. Why would they need to know? Surely, it could be built so discreetly that even Sarah wouldn't technically *have* to know it existed. In the event of a zombie attack, I'd let everyone in, of course. But until that time came, theoretically, I could stay down there for days, and no one would be the wiser. Not that I could get away with days realistically speaking, but an hour here and an hour there…

What wasn't to love about this idea?

"This is what I want." I tapped my finger on the screen. "Absolutely. No, not want. This is what I *need*."

Lou nodded, seeming to be impressed by my decisiveness. Already this bunker was making me a better version of myself. "You want me to draw up the plans for it and provide the estimate?"

"Yep." I nodded, downing some of my chai, not caring too much that it was scorching hot. I'd probably lost a layer off my tongue, but nothing could take away from the sudden hope surging through me right then.

"You don't want to show Sarah these plans first?" Lou pressed, tapping fingers on the tabletop nervously. "I had hoped she'd be here."

"No, she's at work. And…" I rooted around in my brain for something that would end this line of questioning for good. I was too close to the prize right now to let it slip away. "Actually, this is a surprise for her, and I would really like to keep it on the downlow."

"A surprise?" From the way Lou was frowning, I got the impression she did not consider a survival-bunker-slash-panic-room to be a suitable gift for one's spouse.

"As you know, we have four kids. Sometimes we need more… uh," I stumbled, not sure where to go with this, finally settling on, "privacy. You know?"

At first, Lou's confusion deepened, but then a ghost of a smile appeared, followed by a deep-throated chuckle. "Ah, yeah. I got you."

"You do?" By her reaction, I was starting to doubt that she did.

"This is like a Fifty Shades thing." From the way Lou's eyes sparkled with mischief, I was fairly certain she was picturing something very different from what I had in mind.

"Fifty, uh, shades?" I choked a little on my words.

I knew Fifty Shades. I'd actually read the books to find out why Sarah enjoyed them so much. And I didn't hate them, which hurt the snob in me. To be fully honest, the series had even spiced up our sex lives for a bit. But, did Lou think I wanted her to build a sex bunker?

From that sly grin she was wearing, I was pretty certain she did.

I had two options. I could either correct her and admit I was trying to pull a fast one over on my wife by building a secret room where only I could go to escape—which was maybe a little bit psychotic sounding, at least if someone didn't know me. Or I could go along with it and let the contractor's imagination wander to places I probably couldn't even comprehend. Option one was out of the question, but option two seemed harmless enough, so I decided to roll with it.

"You see why I want to keep this quiet for now?" I figured this answer would ensure Lou wouldn't breathe a word to Sarah.

"I like the way you think, Lizzie." Lou fixed me

with an approving gaze. "And hey, if there *is* a zombie apocalypse, you'll be all set. Two birds, one stone."

Now, I had a real conundrum. If Lou found out the truth, she might not respect me, which was odd, because she really liked the idea of the sex bunker. Considering how prudish our society was, I would've assumed that type of thing would be a deal breaker. What would she think if she knew I simply wanted a space away from my family? A place no one could ever violate? Having a bunker no one knew a thing about—it was the best plan I'd come up with in a very long time. Honestly, while I'd liked the idea when Lou first brought it up, I wasn't one hundred percent committed to the idea. Not until I saw the invisible bunker.

Maybe saw wasn't the right word, considering that not seeing it was the whole point. Whatever. All that mattered was I found my Lizzie spot in the house.

I got out my phone and texted Rose, letting her know the meeting was ending, and there was no need to drop by. I had it all under control.

CHAPTER FOURTEEN

I STARED AT ALL THE BOXES IN THE BACK OF my SUV. This had been my fifth party in two weeks. Having friends was turning into an expensive endeavor. Not only did I now have seven large bottles of cleaning supplies—some of them from a different brand than what Tracy had used, but apparently her preferred organic cleaner wasn't the only game in town—I also had a dozen new kitchen gadgets I had no clue how to use. I wasn't even sure what they were supposed to do, except apparently pamper me as I used them.

There was some Tupperware we didn't really need, too. And a pair of leggings. A quilted handbag even a grandmother wouldn't have wanted to use. I'd had no idea that when people threw parties in Massachusetts, it was customary to sell things. Moving to the east coast was turning out to be like moving to a completely foreign culture. I wondered if that was the real reason Sarah had all those Tory Burch tunics. Had Ingrid been selling them at playdates?

Construction had started on the basement, which is to say demolition was well under way, and the entire space looked like a disaster. Frankly, the resemblance to a war zone was a daily reminder of why my secret bunker was such a good idea. It was close to the end of the workday, and I was waiting outside for Lou and her crew to leave. I had a very narrow window in which to hide all this crap from my trunk before Sarah saw me.

Not that I had to justify my purchases to my wife, but it's possible I may have bought more than I'd intended. There was always a deal if you bought a little more. Buy two spatulas and get a whisk! Just one more pair of leggings and the hostess gets a free gift! Let me tell you, for a bunch of suburban moms, those ladies really knew how to upsell. I was a little afraid what Sarah would say if she saw my stash. After all, she'd managed to attend playdates and mom parties for years without this type of thing happening to her. Yet another sign she was better at this than I was.

Luckily for me, down in the basement behind the barrier that still gave access to the makeshift podcast space was a perfect hiding spot. It was the one part of the basement that was off-limits to everyone but Willow and me. Willow wasn't the type to ask too many questions, unlike Sarah who would want to know why I had so many boxes, and did I even know what a spatula was for.

Apparently, the crew was working overtime today. The problem was, Sarah, her mom, and the kids were expected home any second, and I needed time to unload the boxes.

If Lou asked me what was in the boxes, I didn't have to answer, really. She was working for me, not vice versa. What was the worst that would happen? Lou would witness me hiding this stuff. Better her than my wife, who had a sixth sense when I was up to no good. Aside from the bunker situation, which was a masterpiece of good planning on my end, Sarah didn't have an inkling about what was really going on. Yes, there was the tiny wrinkle involving Lou, who kept sending me ideas for a BDSM lair. I'd come up with a solution, though. Every time she sent something, I responded that it wasn't exactly what I had in mind but to keep looking. The woman was persistent. I'd give her that.

I checked the time. It really was now or never, so I bucked up my nerve to handle Lou if she stumbled upon me. Trying to cut down on the number of trips, I stacked three of the boxes up to my eyeballs, making it difficult to see over, so I had to crane my neck to see around.

"Whoa!" I said when the top box started to slide

precariously to the left, forcing me to adjust to get it out of the danger zone. Only for it to shift perilously to the right.

Why did people insist I have friends? It'd added nothing but complications if you asked me, not that anyone bothered to ask me.

On the third and final run, after not bumping into Lou, a miracle in itself, Lou came outside.

"Need help?"

Busted.

"Nope," I said quickly, hoping she'd move along and forget she'd seen anything at all. "I got it. You must be beat. Don't worry about me."

"Is this for the sex dungeon?" she whispered the last part, and I kind of wanted to die.

"Uh, yes." This was not a lie. Ideally, everything I'd bought would be stored there. It wasn't like our kitchen didn't need another whisk, even if it had been free, but the bunker would. I planned to have a full kitchenette installed as soon as I figured out how to convince Lou we needed it for something kinky involving food. My thinking was in case of the zombies, we wouldn't have time to grab essentials, like the thingamajig that turned squash into spaghetti. Not that I would eat that. I hated veggies, even if you tried calling it pasta. I wasn't born yesterday.

"Oooh, do I need to install it?" Her excitement made me squirm.

She seemed really excited about the prospect. I had to give her credit for going above and beyond.

"Not yet, but you'll be the first person I come to when it's time." I had no clue what I meant by this. Maybe the zombie apocalypse would come sooner than expected, and I wouldn't have to figure it out.

Sarah pulled into the driveway, with Rose in the passenger seat.

If it hadn't been for our super helpful contractor, I would have made it without any issues, but no, I had to hire the one contractor on the planet who liked extra work.

"What's all that?" Sarah asked, opening the back door of her SUV. "Calvin, get moving."

The other three kids trooped by with serious faces.

"What happened to ice cream?" I asked.

"Ask Calvin." Sarah snapped her fingers and gave her mom glare to our youngest.

Calvin zipped out of Sarah's car, running past me, disappearing into the house.

Could I do that without raising too much suspicion?

"You didn't answer my question."

Lou and I exchanged nervous glances.

Rose of all people said, "Leave the poor woman alone. Did you once think Lizzie skipped going to ice cream because she's working on a surprise for you?"

Sarah's expression brightened by the thought. I'll

admit I was impressed by Rose's ability to save my butt by thinking on her feet. I wondered if she would find squash spaghetti an acceptable surprise. Which, to reiterate, I did not.

Rose steered Sarah past me. Before they stepped inside, Rose looked over her shoulder and gave me an exaggerated wink. Conspiratorial, even. What the hell was that all about?

When the coast was clear, Lou wiped her forehead with the back of her hand in the universal close call sign.

"You lucked out in the mother-in-law department. Mine is a true nightmare."

I nodded, knowing she was right, even if I was a little surprised by how quickly Lou had determined this, given that she'd never met Rose before. "There was a time whenever I was around Rose she made car revving sounds because she wanted to run me over with her car."

"How'd you get her to change her mind?"

I shrugged. "Life, relationships, and family are a perpetual mystery to me."

"Ain't that the truth? Well, see ya Monday." Lou did a snappy salute that was cooler than cool.

Would it be weird to ask her how to do it her way and not my way that made me look so foolish that Ollie instantly labelled me as annoying?

I decided to save that request for a different day.

My arms were burning from holding two boxes filled with kitchen gadgets and cleaning supplies. Learning how to salute like a cool chick was a project for when I had the time and patience, which I never had. Perhaps when Calvin graduated from college.

CHAPTER FIFTEEN

"Okay, peeps, Sarah will be home soon. Everyone in their places." I glanced around the room, making eye contact with all of my family members, who seemed confused by my directions. "I mean no talking or moving until Sarah walks through that door. This is a surprise party."

"What if I have to pee?" Maddie asked.

"Hold it. There's her car. Kids, unfurl the sign."

The kids gaped at me. Apparently, *unfurl* was not a common vocabulary word for the under six crowd.

"Spread it out so Mommy can read it." I motioned for them to roll out the homemade sign, just to be sure my meaning was clear.

They nodded. Fred and Olivia positioned themselves on the ends, taking careful steps until all of it was visible.

"Hello?" Sarah called out as she entered the house. "Anyone home? Why are the lights off?"

Sarah rounded the corner, and we all yelled, "Surprise!"

"What the fuck?" She clutched her shirt over her heart. It was at this moment I realized I may have made a tactical error.

"Fuck!" Olivia repeated at the top of her lungs, hopping up and down. "Fuck, fuck, fuck!"

The kids were all joining in now like it was some sort of playground nursery rhyme.

"No, Olivia. Surprise. We're surprising Mommy," I said, hoping to redirect our most precocious child. The ringleader, as I liked to think of her.

"Surprise me?" Sarah said with a shaky laugh. "I think you're trying to kill me. It's not my birthday."

"It's for your job, Mommy," Fred explained with a serious expression on his little face that made him look like an old man.

Sarah slanted her head, nearly perpendicular to the floor, taking a second longer to read the sign the kids had made themselves. The letters didn't exactly spell congrats, but *co-rats*. I wasn't sure which kid added the hyphen in hopes of saving the sign. Sarah, though, figured it out, and her eyes started to water. "Kiddos, this is so sweet!"

"Kids, what did we practice all day? On three. One, two, three!" I snapped my fingers on the last count.

"We're proud of you, Mommy!"

Sarah hunched down, putting her arms out to hug all four of them. "I love you wonderful people." She straightened and put her arms around me. "And, I heart you."

"Ditto." I squeezed her tightly.

"Spread the love." Maddie elbowed me in the side. "We're so proud of you."

My heart raced like a hyperactive cat, bursting across the room and sliding into a wall, but I forced my mind not to think how drastically things would change in the fall when we both worked full-time. Sarah wanted to go back to work, and I wanted her to be happy. That meant making sacrifices. At least, all the kids would be in school in September since the younger two would be starting preschool. Sarah had even talked me into having them go full day to hopefully get caught up on the missed years due to COVID.

"Oh, we need to do back-to-school shopping!" I whacked my head, forgetting that detail.

"We have a few weeks," Sarah reassured me. "School only just got out."

"I could go with you," my dad offered, confusing the heck out of me. "I love a good food court."

If my father's offer to go shopping stunned me into silence, the food court comment nearly knocked me flat on my ass. Charles Allen Petrie eating at a mall food court? This was a sight I would pay to see.

"He means the Cheesecake Factory," Helen clarified.

"That makes more sense," I replied. It didn't make a lot more sense, given how snobbish my dad was, but my brain was still circling the airport, waiting for a place to land.

"Cheesecake?" Allen, my youngest brother, piped up. "Are we having cheesecake?"

"When we go back-to-school shopping," my father clarified.

Was the whole family going to go? If that was the case, could I stay home? I hated shopping.

It struck me that instead of displaying the same shock I'd felt, Allen simply nodded, like this was a normal thing my dad would do. Then it hit me. My dad had probably gone back-to-school shopping with Allen, who'd been his secret love child until a few years ago. My brain still grappled with that. Along with my heart. But, my father had been working on repairing our relationship, even moving across the country to be close to me and the grandkids.

Maddie opened a bottle of bubbly while Willow opened sparkling cider so the kids—and I—wouldn't feel left out.

After everyone had a glass, the little ones drinking out of plastic cups, Rose cleared her throat. "To my darling daughter. You've constantly made me proud. Your huge heart and desire to make a difference in the world. And courage. May all of your children and students take after you."

"Cheers!" Everyone raised their glasses. Including

me, even if I couldn't help thinking Rose's wish that all the children took after Sarah was mostly because otherwise they would take after me. Honestly, that was fair. I wouldn't wish being like me on any of them.

Soon enough, the hubbub of the party gave me cover to step to the side and take stock of things.

"You okay?" Willow asked.

"Yep. Oh, hey. I need to get a gift for Sarah. Do you have any ideas?"

"What's the occasion? For the party?" Willow's brow furrowed as if she didn't want to tell me if that was the case, I was too late.

I didn't want to confess it was because Sarah thought I'd already purchased her a surprise gift when I was trying to get away with sneaking all the junk from my trunk into the bunker I couldn't admit I had, so instead I said, "Just cause."

"Aw, that's sweet," Willow said with a touch of wistfulness in her tone. "Maddie never gets me a gift for no reason."

"Do you get her one?"

"Actually, no." Willow's face scrunched as she pondered her answer. "I think I will now. Is that the secret to a good relationship? Showing the other every day how much they matter, not simply on the big milestones?"

"Yeah, absolutely." I really hoped Willow didn't find out the truth, that I was only covering my buttocks. I didn't want to burst her bubble with proof that I wasn't someone to admire.

I forced down some of the sparkling cider to push the lump of guilt to the pit of my stomach. It felt about as pleasant as it sounded.

Willow rejoined the party, and my father switched places with her with such orchestrated speed I wondered if the whole family would take a turn babysitting me, the grumpy one, in the corner.

"How can Helen and I help in the fall?"

"What do you mean?"

"We know you and Sarah will be running around like chickens with your heads cut off. Helen and I were thinking of picking up the kids on Tuesday and Thursday for time with us."

"Every Tuesday and Thursday?" I nearly choked on my drink.

"Yes. You teach those days, right?"

"I do." I almost followed up with, "How'd you know that?" since this was the man who was pretty much nonexistent my entire childhood. Hence, why I'd had a nanny. Belatedly, it struck me that my father might know a thing or two about the topic, so I asked, "What do you think of nannies?"

"Come again?"

"Sarah wants us to hire a nanny, and I've been resistant." *Please don't ask why*, I thought. There was no way to explain I'd feel like a failure of a parent without implying I thought he was.

"I know you want to be everything for your children," he said cautiously, "and I admire that, but sometimes you have to admit you need help. There's no shame in that, Lizzie. It took me a year and many attempts to find you the right nanny."

"What? I only ever had Annie."

"She was the fifth if I remember correctly."

My mouth dropped open. "I had five nannies? That's not possible."

He laughed. "The others were short-lived. I wanted nothing but the best for you. I knew I wasn't the greatest dad, but your nanny had to be the best."

"You're doing pretty good now," I admitted, my eyes tearing up more than I wanted to admit. "What kind of cheesecake do you like?" I asked to steer us away from full-on waterworks. This was Sarah's party, and breaking down in tears seemed like a foul.

"Classic, of course."

I had to laugh because, of course, that was what he would say. I couldn't imagine my father trying some outrageous flavor. Then again, he was really coming into himself these days, so who knew how often he'd surprise me? It warmed my heart, really. Not only could my dad relax some, but perhaps I had that ability as well.

CHAPTER SIXTEEN

Three nights later, I stood in my bedroom so exhausted I contemplated crawling under the covers and not bothering to change out of my shorts and T-shirt. With no warning, Sarah stormed in with the energy of a Category 5 hurricane.

"You're building a sex dungeon?" Sarah had a hand on her hip, and her screech could've woken the dead.

"I'm what?" It wasn't my best stalling tactic. But for one thing, I was tired. And for another, how the hell did she know about that? Sure, I knew there was a chance my secret cover story would get blown, but I hadn't expected to be asked about it with such bluntness, and especially not when my mind was complete jelly. I probably couldn't count to fifteen without using my fingers and toes.

"And you told my mom you're building it. My *mother*, Lizzie. She gave birth to me!"

"I never said such a thing to your mother!" I countered with all the righteous indignation I was entitled to. As an afterthought, I added, "It's not even a real sex dungeon."

"What is it, then? Because from the drawings I've seen, it's a naughty play room that Christian Grey would salivate over."

"Drawings? What drawings? I haven't seen any drawings." Had I missed a memo or something? What would the subject line even have said? Maybe it had said "Sex Dungeon," and my spam filter had sent it to the same place as the *FRee V!@gra* offers.

"These drawings." Without further ado, Sarah shoved her iPad into my hands.

"What the…?" I didn't understand anything my eyes were registering. Truthfully, they were so tired, everything blurred. But there was a lot of red. And black. Like an illustration of Satan's bedroom. "How did this get onto your tablet? Are we going to be on a weird watch list now? One for pervs?" I whispered the last line, glancing nervously at the smart speaker on Sarah's bedside that I was absolutely convinced tracked everything we said and did.

"This is *my* fault?" Sarah whacked my shoulder with her palm. "You're the one who's been keeping secrets from me. But not from my fucking mother. When it comes to sex chambers, that's a secret you should absolutely keep from my fucking mother."

"I wish you'd stop saying fucking mother, because

under the current circumstances, it's tormenting me." I tapped the side of my head to prevent images from forming.

"Yeah, okay. And you say I'm the perv. You need to explain everything to me right fucking now." Sarah planted her feet, crossed her arms, and glared at me.

"I don't even know how or where to start." This was one hundred percent true.

"That's a pattern for you, FYI. Why don't you tell me what's really going on in the basement? I knew I shouldn't have trusted you with the project, but I never thought it would get this out of hand. At worst, I thought you'd add a hot tub or something. I still can't believe that you're creating a sex club in our house, where our kids sleep?"

"Sex club? How did it morph into a sex club all of a sudden? I don't even like clubs."

"Apparently, a lot of people do. Like my mother and Troy, as it turns out. My mom has assured me they would pay top dollar to use such a room."

"Really? How much?" As soon as I said it, I knew it was the worst possible response.

"What?" As Sarah shrieked, I thought I felt something deep inside my ear canal go *pop*. "Please God, tell me you don't have any fancy brochures printed up yet."

"No. One, it's not a sex club, dungeon, or chamber of any kind, and two"—I made a V in the air with my fingers—"I didn't want anyone to know about the room. No one. Aside from Lou and her crew, but she promised not to breathe a word about it. Oh my God. I just realized your mom must've shown up to that coffee shop meeting right after I left, even though I told her not to."

"Of course, she did. Since when would she take your word for it that you had things under control?"

"Good point. I bet Lou spilled the beans when she showed up. We should fire her."

"Heads are going to roll, but not Lou's." Sarah took a menacing step closer to me.

"It's a bunker, okay? A fucking bunker—no, not for fucking," I corrected when the meaning of my words became clear. "It's for me. To have privacy. And in case the world ends, it's someplace we all can live. I wanted a bunker. Nothing more. Nothing less. I'm suffocating!" To add drama to my statement, I started to hyperventilate. Between ragged breaths, I wheezed out, "I… need breaks. I can't go a day without s-some silence." I sat on the edge of the bed, trying to calm my breathing. "I'm sorry. I know I'm a terrible person because I don't always want to be around my family twenty-four hours a day, seven days a week. I don't know what's wrong with me, but I need space sometimes. Like thirty minutes a day in absolute quiet because when I don't get it, I want to scream and cry. I don't want to be the screaming banshee mother. I want to be a loving and supportive parent, but I can't always be that way when I don't get breaks."

"That I understand. I love the she-shed you gave me for exactly that reason. Why don't you use it, too?"

"It's your spot. I wanted my own spot."

"A bunker." Sarah sat down next to me with a shallow sigh. "I mean, it does fit your personality. I remember your desire to build a moat around our house."

"I might go back to that idea." I smacked my hand hard against the duvet. "I can't even trust Lou. Everyone twists everything I say or do."

Sarah raised an eyebrow. "Do you think you play a role in that?"

"Probably, but…" I didn't know how to defend myself because was there a defense? Out of eight billion people in the world, I seemed to be the only one who got into these scrapes with such regularity.

"What I don't get," Sarah said, "is how Lou got it in her head you were building a sex dungeon."

"Uh, I told her not to tell you about the hidden space. It's highly possible she misconstrued my reason for wanting to keep it quiet." I put both my hands defensively in front of my face. "Yes, I knew she thought I had that in mind for the space, but I have no idea why she told your mother. Who tells someone's mother-in-law something like that?"

"Who tells their hot contractor something like that?" Sarah mimicked.

I bristled. "She's not hot."

"Lou is most definitely hot."

I frowned, turning this information over in my mind. I supposed Sarah was right, though I'd never really given it any thought. "Is it somehow my fault that she's attractive? I thought she was going to be a hairy butt crack guy."

"Yeah, so did I. But no, it's not your fault. I don't know how you get into these messes, but—" She started to laugh. "Can I confess something? Mad as I was, I'm a little disappointed it's not a sex dungeon. You have to admit our sexy times have been few and far between lately."

"Do I really have to admit that?" I felt like I was walking into a trap.

"You know it's true, and if you think I'm trying to trick you, I'm not. It's just—I could have lived a long, happy life never knowing my mom was the type who wants to frequent sex clubs."

"It's hard to picture Troy, the 'Twinkle Twinkle Little Star' fanatic, spanking your mother." Naturally, as soon as I said this, it became almost impossible not to picture it. In fact, all I could see was Troy smacking Rose's bottom in time to the song.

It turned out there was a hell, and I'd arrived.

Sarah stuck her fingers into her ears and pinched her eyes shut. "If you ever want to have sex with me again, never say anything like that ever."

"Don't get mad at me. At least my mom isn't causing issues for once." The woman would have a lot to say on the topic, nothing good in all probability since she loved to refer to me as a les-bi-an, but she'd been dead for years.

"Don't curse us. It's just what we need. Your mother's ghost haunting our sex dungeon."

"I'm not building a sex dungeon!" I tossed my hands in the air.

"That's where you're wrong," Sarah said with a lascivious grin. "You are now. I've suffered too much not to get something out of this venture."

"Back up there a second. You're not going to cancel the bunker?"

"No. But it's not a bunker. It's a space for privacy. For you. And, I'm hoping you invite me in once in a while for kinky sex." She added, "Before Lou starts that part of the project, though, I want to go over the proposal and see how much it's going to cost."

Considering all the various ways this conversation could have ended, this was one I could more than live with.

CHAPTER SEVENTEEN

"Lizzie, can you join me in the basement?" Sarah whizzed through the front room where I sat watching a movie with the kids. When I didn't jump into action instantly, Sarah snapped her fingers.

"Listen to the boss," Fred said, giggling, hiding his face behind Ollie.

"She's your boss, too." I muttered as I got to my feet. "Coming, boss lady." I put a finger to my lips, smiling at all four kids.

Sarah waited at the top of the stairs. "Is that my new nickname?"

"Did you hear that? It's an inside joke with the kiddos."

"I want a name tag that says that so all of you know I'm in charge." She winked at me. "Lou needs to talk to us."

"You know, that's almost as bad as when you say

we have to talk. Every time we talk to Lou, another decimal place gets added to the estimate."

"Says the bunker lady."

Lou stood with two of her crew members, going over a plan. She smiled warmly when she spotted us, but I remained wary. "Just the ladies I wanted to speak to."

"Reporting for duty!" I saluted. I was pretty sure I'd nailed the cool factor this time.

Sarah laughed, making it clear I had not. Good thing for me she wasn't bothered I was being such a goofball. "You need to stop doing that."

"It's kinda fun, but I can't get the snap of my wrist right." I tried again.

"It's more like this." Lou demonstrated.

I made another attempt but didn't quite pull it off. Lou stood behind me, placing one hand on my hip and using her other hand to take mine to do the motion for me.

"Hey, I think I got it now." I whirled around and saluted Sarah. "What do you think? Better?"

Sarah didn't seem to know what to say, and that was when I remembered Sarah saying Lou was hot. And, said hot woman just had her hands on me. Whoops!

"What'd you need me—us—for?" I asked Lou, suddenly eager to change the subject, even if it did cost me another thousand bucks.

"It's time for us to demolish the closet, and before

we take a sledge hammer to it, I wanted to ask if there's anything in there."

"I'm pretty sure we emptied that during the pandemic." Sarah took three steps to the door to open it, but I rushed around her and spread my hands and legs out to block her.

"Don't!" I exclaimed on the off chance she didn't understand my *do not enter* body language.

Sarah and Lou exchanged a *holy cow* look. Now I was in trouble.

"This is why I never open a room or closet without a client being present," Lou explained to Sarah, ignoring me. I wondered if this was true, or if she thought this closet was where I was stashing all our kinky sex toys.

If only.

"Lizzie, darling," Sarah spoke softly, but I wasn't fooled. She was doing her best not to flip her lid. "Can you move aside so I can see what's going on?"

"No can do. It'll ruin the surprise."

Sarah put a hand on each of my shoulders and moved me out of the way like I was one of the kids. "After the bunker news, I no longer like surprises."

"You canned the bunker." I finagled my way back in front of the closet. It was true. A day after saying we could keep the bunker, Sarah had somehow talked me into remodeling the garage with a studio apartment instead, which was considerably cheaper, but it still stung. All of this, and I didn't even get a bunker.

"I told you we needed a living space above the garage, and we can't afford both. I had no idea bunkers were so expensive. We've talked about this. Now move, or someone's going to get hurt, and it won't be me."

I glanced over Sarah's shoulder toward Lou who put two hands in the air, signifying I was on my own.

"I can explain," I blurted.

Sarah opened the door, exposing the boxes of crap I'd been stashing in the closet all summer. "What is this?"

"Uh, all-purpose cleanser?" I replied as she tapped one of the bottles with her toe.

"There must be ten bottles of it. And it says concentrate. Jesus, this is enough for a hundred years. Is this a vegetable spiralizer?" She didn't stop for an answer, tucking that box under her arm and rummaging for more evidence to hold against me in a court of law. "This box says it's a microwave s'more maker." She tapped it, giving me her *you need to explain this shit right fucking now* glare.

"I was stocking up for the bunker. It's not my fault you closed that construction project down. We were well on our way of being fully stocked for the end of the world."

"Because no one can survive the end of the world without a s'mores maker?"

"The world might be over, but do we have to suffer?" was my retort.

Lou tried stifling a snicker but did not succeed. I was pretty sure Lou was on my side.

"What about this?" Sarah continued to rummage through the stuff to pull out an item I'd completely forgotten about. "It's a quilted travel bag. Where will you be traveling to after the world ends?"

"Uh, other bunkers, maybe?"

"You wouldn't be caught dead with this, even at the end of the world. It looks like it belongs to a centenarian from Alabama. Stop lying."

"I'm going to check on the crew." Lou skedaddled, and I wished I could follow.

"I'm not… not really… it's just…" I spluttered, struggling with how to put the problem into words. The best I could manage was, "This is really all your fault."

Sarah squeezed the travel bag like it was my neck. "Oh, this I can't wait to hear."

"You told me to make friends."

Sarah's eyes fluttered like something had gotten into them, but she didn't do anything to clear the debris out. "And?"

"This is what they do here." I gave a weak laugh. "I mean, come on. You know how it is. Look at all your tunics."

"Tunics? What the hell do my tunics—no. Wait." She drew what was probably supposed to be a cleansing breath. It made her nostrils flare like a dragon about to blow fire. "Pretend I have no fucking clue what you're talking about, and walk me through what it is friends do here in Massachusetts that somehow led to this."

"The first party I went to was Tracy's. Except, it wasn't at her house but Jen's. Tracy cleaned Jen's kitchen and then sold the product. Sarah, you should have seen it. Jen's place was a pigsty, and Tracy made it shine. I've been using it in our house, and even you mentioned the kitchen had an extra sparkle."

"Okay…" Sarah wasn't exactly agreeing with me, but she wasn't arguing, either. So far, so good.

"And then it was Cynthia's turn. That was kitchen gadgets, I think. The pampering ones. And then Bonnie had a cocktail party, only there were leggings at that one—"

"Leggings?"

I nodded. "They're in the travel bag."

"I'm too scared to look."

"Yeah, I wouldn't," I agreed. "Anyway, there was another kitchen party, and more cleaning supplies, and they had pigs in a blanket, so I couldn't very well not buy anything. And every time, there were new friends, and they had parties, and then the stuff just kept coming, and.." I ended in a shrug, too overwhelmed to finish my sentence.

"These were all from those parties you went to?" Sarah studied me and then all the junk in the closet. "I don't know how to tell you this, but, Lizzie, you've gotten in deep with a multi-level marketing cult."

"What?" My mouth gaped as I struggled to comprehend what she was saying. "But haven't you been doing the same thing when you have friend night? I assumed you were better at hiding your booty."

"No, this is not at all what we do." Sarah corrected me as gently as she could considering she was staring at maybe a grand worth of shit we couldn't even use in a bunker, thanks to that not being a thing we were doing anymore. "We do normal friend things. Have dinner. Drink wine. Go for walks. Chat."

"I don't understand. Every time I've gotten together with my friends, it's involved a sales pitch. I think they're wondering about what product I'll start selling. Jen's been hinting we need an Avon lady in the group."

Sarah pressed her fingers into her forehead. "I can't believe I have to say this, but you can't be an Avon lady. You don't even wear makeup."

"Tell me something I don't know. It's why I've been hedging, but they're not going to want to be my friends if I don't up my game and soon." I tossed in begrudgingly, "I like hanging out with them. You were right about that."

"I'm happy to hear that, but you don't have to buy things from them to keep them as friends. Rather, if you do, then they're really not your friends. That's not what friendship is."

"How can you say that with a straight face?" I demanded. "Even the kids wouldn't buy that line."

"They should because it's true. You cannot keep buying this crap. It's got to be a couple thousand dollars of stuff we don't need."

"Can we try the s'mores maker? I've been wanting to give that one a whirl. And, those leggings are soft. You might like them." I reached around Sarah, fishing for them.

"Yes, we can have s'mores, but promise me, Lizzie. No more of these parties."

"I'll be back to square one, though," I argued. "Need I remind you, you didn't like me then? I'll end up with no friends and you not liking me, wondering when I'll be served divorce papers." I was close to tears.

Sarah wrapped her arms around me. "Everything's going to be fine. Tracy doesn't seem like a con artist. I have absolutely no desire to divorce you, believe it or not. Too expensive, and you just spent all our savings on pyramid schemes." She cracked a smile, but I didn't.

"I feel like an idiot."

"I'm sure it'll all work out." Sarah made cooing sounds like when she used to rock a crying baby. It was kind of nice.

CHAPTER EIGHTEEN

THE KIDS TUMBLED OUT OF THE SUV, EXCITED for the puppet show birthday party, but I would rather have been skinny dipping with piranhas.

Sarah tossed an arm around my neck. "It's going to be fine."

"How? Tracy's going to be here, and you said I had to break up with her."

"I said you have to say no more multi-level marketing parties. You can still be friends."

"Why would anyone want to be friends with me? I'm an odd ball." I held the door open for Sarah. "If I'm not buying things from them, I fail to see what they get out of it."

"You're Lizzie, an amazing woman with a quirky sense of humor."

"Quirky is a synonym for odd ball, ya know." I wasn't convinced of this, but I hoped she got my point.

"So is funky, and you like it when we get funky in the sheets," she whispered into my ear.

"We're at a birthday party," I scolded as a delicious chill snaked down my spine. How was it that we could go so long without actually having sex, and yet every time we were at a child's birthday party—the least inappropriate place on the planet for this kind of thing—this evil vixen I was married to managed to get me all hot and bothered? I set the wrapped gift on the table with all the other gifts. "By the way, this gift giving thing in the course of the year probably costs as much as my parties. How are these different?"

"Buying a gift for a child for their birthday is not a pyramid scheme. I can't believe I have to explain this to you."

There was a commotion in the room that prevented me from responding. Probably for my own good.

"Okay, kids, get in line to draw a number." Sarah pointed to the back of the line.

"What for?" I asked, not sure if I should be excited or suspicious. "Do I need a number?"

"It's for the magical chest, and no, you don't get to win a prize."

"Adulting sucks. You know that? I'm done adulting." I took a seat next to Sarah in the back, crossing my arms and pouting to drive home I was serious about what I'd said. There would be zero adult behavior from me today. She could count on that.

The kids got their numbers for the drawing and

then sat in the first couple of rows for the puppet show to start. Can I mention how much I firmly believe puppet shows are bonkers? Like, they're fucking puppets. They have strings and yarn for hair. Who actually believes the action is happening for real?

All the kids, apparently. They seemed thoroughly entertained. That made me wonder if I could ever really reclaim childhood enchantment and ditch the reality of adulting once and for all. I think adulthood had ruined me for it. Twenty minutes later, I was ready to pull the rip cord. No way could I go back to childhood. I didn't enjoy it when I was a kid, and I certainly wouldn't now.

"How much longer?" I whispered into Sarah's ear, one eye firmly glued to the exit sign above the door.

She responded by pinching my thigh.

It didn't really answer my question, but it did stop me from asking again. However, I gave her the stink eye.

After what seemed like seven years and four days, a woman dressed like a court jester clapped her hands. Seriously, what was up with court jesters and heralds at parties? When I was a kid, I don't ever remember needing to engage in some delusion that I was royalty. Kids these days.

"Are you ready to find out who's going to help Roger open the magical chest?" the jester asked.

The children squealed in delight.

What in the world was going on? Why did Roger need help opening a chest? Was it stuck?

The woman pulled out a number from a box. "The winner is seventeen."

"That's me!" Calvin jumped up and down. I'd be lying if I said I wasn't a little bit jealous, even if I had no idea what was happening or what he'd won. I never won anything.

"Come on up." The woman motioned for my youngest to join her. "Here's your key. Now you unlock this one." She patted the lefthand side. "Roger, the birthday boy, will unlock this one. On the count of three."

The kids counted down.

Calvin and Roger turned their keys.

I'm gonna be honest. I don't think the locks were real. They looked like they were made of papier-mâché and painted with poster paints. And the keys were ridiculously oversized. Magical locks, my ass.

The woman opened the chest, which had definitely never been locked. "Baby Yodas!" She took out one plush Baby Yoda and handed it to Roger. Then she gave an identical one to Calvin.

"Does she know it's not Calvin's birthday?"

Sarah shooshed me. I thought it was a reasonable question. If Roger's parents expected us to pitch in for the cost of this party, they had a rude awakening coming their way.

"Now for the rest of the kids, come get your surprises."

All the kids lined up, each one taking a smaller Baby Yoda from the so-called magical chest. When the last one got theirs, Sarah motioned for us to get up.

"Cake time?" I asked, excited. That was the only reason to have a birthday party in my book.

"Soon. Oh, look. Tracy's getting punch. Will you get me a cup of punch?" Sarah didn't wait for a reply, shoving me toward Tracy.

Real subtle, Sarah.

"This is an odd party," I said, scooping some punch out of the bowl and wishing I could dunk my head in it and drown.

"It's much better than the one last week," Tracy replied. "All Joe Junior got was a cheap yo-yo that didn't last a day. He's thrilled with his Baby Yoda." Tracy smiled at her son, who was chatting away with Fred. "Have you RSVP'd to Marsha's party?"

"About that." I sipped Sarah's punch, my heart pounding and sweat beading on my palms. "Um, I can't go to the parties anymore."

Tracy's face fell. "Why not?"

"Sarah found my stash, and she's put her foot down." I didn't feel bad at all blaming Sarah since that was indeed what she'd done.

Instead of storming off in a huff, Tracy actually looked sympathetic. "I remember when Joe found my boxes."

"Mad?" I guessed.

"Hopping. Why do you think I started selling the cleaning products? He wouldn't let me go to parties anymore unless I at least started selling enough to cover the costs. You need to start."

I shook my head. "I've been told that's a hard no, as well. Besides, it was getting expensive, and if we're all doing it so we can hang out, why don't we just hang out and not work?"

"Sure," Tracy said with a nonchalant shrug. "We can do that."

I started to point out the benefit, but her words sunk in. "You mean we can go to dinner or for a walk and not buy stuff?"

"Absolutely. Actually, I'm having people over next weekend for trivia night. Do you like Trivial Pursuit?"

"That's a game I can play." I almost hugged her. I couldn't believe I wasn't being shunned. "I hate Pictionary and charades."

"Those games give me the willies." She shook all about, and I laughed, knowing exactly how she felt. We were definitely on the same page, me and her. Like, well, friends. "We're ordering pizza."

"Should I bring anything?"

"I won't turn down wine," Tracy said with a grin.

"That, I can do," I promised.

Joe Junior was waving to get Tracy's attention. "See ya Saturday."

I saluted, making her laugh. It was like we were friendship soulmates.

Sarah sidled up next to me. "You're not going to stop that ridiculous salute, are you?"

"Not now," I vowed. "I can finally salute without looking like a dork."

Sarah sucked her lips into her mouth, giving me the impression she was choking on an unsaid retort. I was too elated with the way the encounter with Tracy had turned out to care.

"When's the cake?" I asked.

"Soon, but how'd it go with Tracy?"

"You'll be happy to know next Saturday I'm going to her house for trivia night. I'm going to clean their clocks," I said, my eyes narrowing in competitive fervor, "unless I get stuck on the sports question. My least favorite."

"You're adorable." Sarah kissed my cheek.

"I think you actually meant it that time."

"I mean it every time, even if I'm annoyed."

I thought about this for a moment. "I prefer when you aren't annoyed."

"Me too," Sarah said, her voice barely above a whisper. "Don't look now, but they're bringing out the cake."

I whipped around, spying the cake. What a glorious day! I even joined in on singing "Happy Birthday." I felt like a new me.

CHAPTER NINETEEN

"You ready?" Sarah had one hand on the door, waiting for me to give her the go-ahead. It was almost the end of summer, and Sarah's skin glowed faintly from several weeks of being in the sun.

I looked at the new addition to the garage and sighed. "I'm sad it's not my bunker."

"Don't give up on your bunker dream." Sarah winked, instantly stirring a response deep inside, in parts of me I'd kind of forgotten existed.

"Really?" I clapped my hands together. "I can have a bunker?"

"Maybe." She winked again, but this time it did not have the same effect.

My shoulders fell. "That always means no."

"It means maybe. Now, are you ready to see the new apartment?"

"Whatever." I rolled my eyes.

She opened the door to the apartment above the garage, immediately oohing and aahing. "It's even better in the daylight."

I stood in the middle of the space, admiring all the natural light, begrudgingly unable to disagree with her. "It is."

"Valentina is going to be happy here."

My brow creased, and I crossed my arms tightly against my chest. "I feel like a human trafficker."

"Don't ever joke about that in public." Sarah wagged a finger in the air. "Do you know how lucky we were to get her? Au pairs have their pick of places this season. The fact she'll have her own apartment is the reason she chose us. Not only will it be great for the kids to learn Spanish, but she'll love going to school here. It's a win-win for everyone."

"Including you." It's possible this was said with a touch of petulance.

"And, you," she pointed out for the hundredth time since she'd gotten me to give in to her au pair plan. "I'm not the only one who works full-time. Do you not remember how much you struggled last semester?"

"I still have nightmares about it." It was true. To this day, I couldn't look at my globe without a sense of dread.

"Everyone's going to love this arrangement."

"What if she kills us in our sleep?"

"I can't believe Lou pulled it off," Sarah continued, ignoring my totally valid question. "Val's arriving tomorrow, just in time for school to start."

"Of course, Lou pulled it off. You took her off the hard project."

"The basement?"

"The bunker."

Again, Sarah ignored me. "She's promising to finish the basement in less than a month. That means Maddie and Willow will be able to move into their own space. The kids will be able to spread out, and you and I will have more alone time." Sarah ran a finger down the side of my face, rekindling some of the sparks from earlier. "In fact, the kids are at your dad's house. Maddie and Willow are in Boston for the night. Shall we?"

"Here?" I gulped.

"Shouldn't someone break it in?" She shimmied up to me, hip checking me. "Let's dance."

"There's no music."

"We can dance to our heartbeats."

"You're in a good mood." I stood still while Sarah did a little jig. I didn't mind the view, that was for certain. She could dance all night, as long as I wasn't expected to join.

"Life is good. Don't you feel it?"

"I'm feeling your boobs pressed into my back." I looked over my shoulder, to stare into her eyes. "If you really want to get lucky, can we go to our room? Not the human trafficking quarters."

Sarah shot a glance at the ceiling that clearly telegraphed *heaven help me* to anyone who might be inclined to respond. "You're impossible."

"So. Are. You." I tapped her nose with the tip of my finger on each word.

Sarah silenced me with a kiss.

I deepened it, while walking Sarah to the door.

"You're no fun."

"I'm not having sex in the au pair's room. That's just wrong."

"She's not here right now."

"Out. Now!" I pointed to the door.

Across the yard at the main house, Lou was on her way out the door. "See ya Monday."

Sarah flicked toodle-loo fingers, while I'm sure my face was going up in flames.

Sarah and I entered the house, and she turned toward the library.

"No. Bed. I need a bed." As if to hammer home the point, my right knee cracked. "I'm almost forty, dear."

"An old spoilsport." Sarah tugged my hand, leading me upstairs.

When we reached the bedroom, I gently shoved Sarah onto the bed.

"I see. You're old, but I can be tossed about."

"You'll always be younger than I am. Always." I climbed on top of Sarah.

"Aren't you forgetting something?"

I thought for a minute. I was probably forgetting all sorts of things. It really had been that long, though I was eager to set the counter back to zero. And not just because I liked ticking things off a list. It really had been much too long.

"It's daylight," I finally guessed, stumped. "I can't turn the lights off."

"Your shirt. Off." Sarah helped me rip it off, almost like she didn't trust me to comply. She needn't have worried.

"You still have yours on," I pointed out helpfully.

"Really? I wonder why." So, in fact, did I. I was still wondering when she cleared her throat and tried in vain to wiggle beneath the weight of my body. "Lizzie? Figure it out."

I stared down at her, finally realizing the issue. I moved to the side to allow her to yank her top and bra off. "It's like I've never had sex before."

"It's been ages," she agreed, peppering kisses along my shoulder.

"I've been reading how it's not healthy for a couple to stop having sex." I sucked in my last word as Sarah licked my neck.

She chuckled against my earlobe, sending sparks flying from my core. "I hope you cleared your internet history."

"I do that regularly." I was distracted by her nibbling, but not too much to forget my bone saw fascination. I grimaced slightly at the idea of someone who didn't know I was harmless stumbling on that one. "Every night, in fact."

"I can't imagine all the things you lock away in here." She cupped my cheek, gazing at me through half-lowered lids.

"It's not pretty."

"I disagree. It's you. I love you. No matter what."

I nuzzled my face into the crook of her neck.

Sarah ran her hand up and down my back.

"I've missed you so much," I said softly, speaking from my heart.

"Show me."

I kissed my way to her lips, staying put for many blissful seconds, before making my way down her chin, neck, along her right shoulder, skipping her arm, because my need was kicking into overdrive, and taking her nipple into my mouth. Sarah let out a gasp.

Not wanting to leave her other nipple out of the action, I teased it with my fingers. Sarah moaned. One of my hands trailing down her side, feeling the goosebumps that multiplied.

It'd been too long.

"Let's not do that again," I said.

"We haven't finished," Sarah said with alarm. "You better not be quitting."

"I meant let's not go this long without connecting. It nearly killed me."

She gazed into my eyes. "Me too."

We made love like it was the first time and we had our whole lives in front of us, and in that moment, I believed that, my heart filling with joy.

A HUGE THANK YOU!

First, thanks so much for reading *A Woman in Hiding.* When I published *A Woman Lost,* which turned out to be my first book series, I had no idea the impact Lizzie would have on so many. I've received countless emails from readers who have confessed how much she means to them. It wasn't until I announced the end of the series that I realized how many love her. I have to admit while it's flattering, it's also intimidating because I fear I'll eventually mess up the Lizzie arc, letting down readers.

However, that's the risk a writer has to take with every single story they publish. And, I feel like I should say this right now. Lizzie's story will continue. Ideas are already percolating in my head, but I have to let them sit a bit before tackling the next installment.

I've published more than twenty-five novels, and I still find it simply amazing that people read my stories.

A HUGE THANK YOU!

When I hit publish on my first book back in 2013, after staring at the publish button for several days before I worked up the nerve to finally press it, I had no idea what would happen.

Years later, I still panic when I'm about to publish a new project, but it's because of your support that I find the courage to do it. My publishing career has been a wonderful journey, and I wouldn't be where I am today without you cheering me on.

If you enjoyed the story, I would really appreciate a review. Even short reviews help immensely.

Finally, don't forget if you want to stay in touch, sign up for my newsletter. I'll send you a free copy of *A Woman Lost* (just in case you don't have it yet), book 1 in the A Woman Lost series, plus the bonus chapters and *Tropical Heat* (a short story), all of which are exclusive to subscribers. And, you'll be able to enter monthly giveaways to win one of my books.

You'll also be one of the firsts to hear about many of my misadventures, like the time I accidentally ordered thirty pounds of oranges, instead of five. To be honest, that stuff happens to me a lot.

Here's the link to join: http://eepurl.com/hhBhXX

And, thanks again for letting Lizzie into your hearts.

ABOUT THE AUTHOR

TB Markinson is an American who's recently returned to the US after a seven-year stint in the UK and Ireland. When she isn't writing, she's traveling the world, watching sports on the telly, visiting pubs in New England, or reading. Not necessarily in that order.

Her novels have hit Amazon bestseller lists for lesbian fiction and lesbian romance. For a full listing of TB's novels, please visit her Amazon page.

On the *Lesbians Who Write* weekly podcast, she and Clare Lydon dish about the good, the bad, and the ugly of writing. TB also runs I Heart SapphFic, a place for authors and fans of lesfic to come together to celebrate and chat about lesbian fiction.

Want to learn more about TB. Hop over to her *About* page on her website for the juicy bits. Okay, it won't be all that titillating, but you'll find out more